15.95

SUPERMAN® FAMILY ADVENTURES™

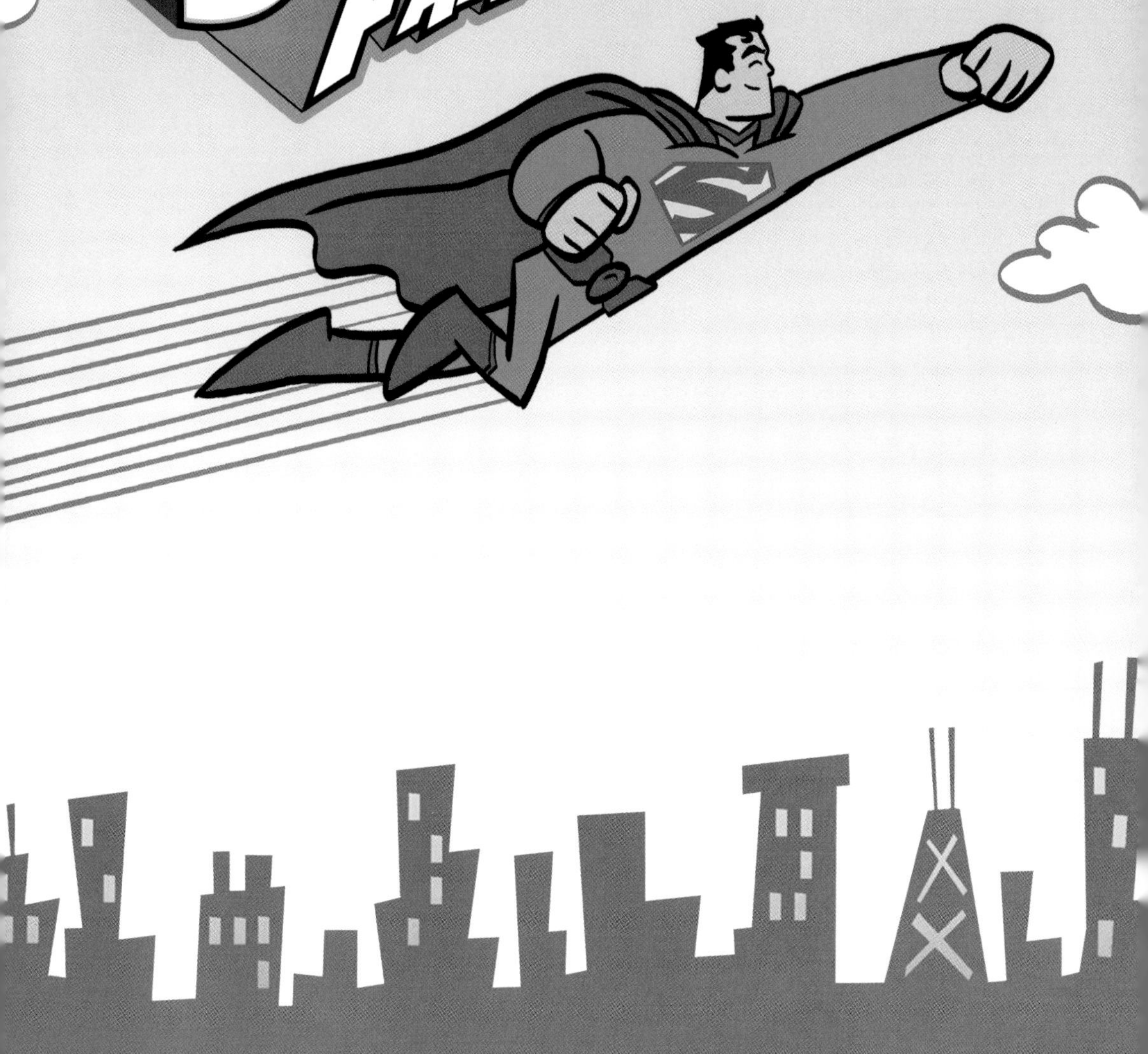

STONE ARCH BOOKS
a capstone imprint

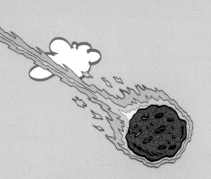

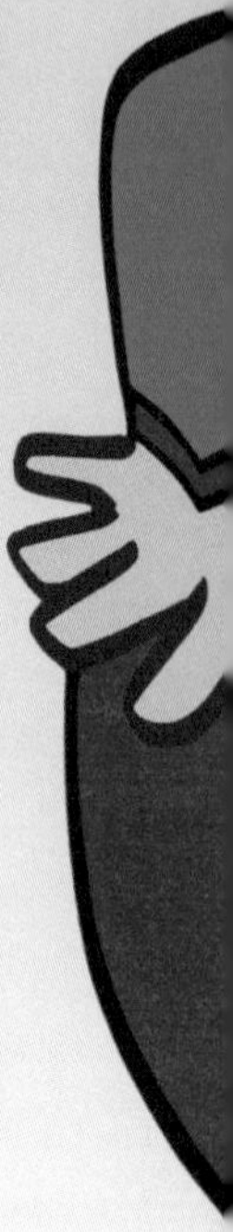

STONE ARCH BOOKS®

Published in 2014
A Capstone Imprint
1710 Roe Crest Drive
North Mankato, MN 56003
www.capstonepub.com

Originally published by DC Comics in the U.S. in single magazine form as SUPERMAN FAMILY ADVENTURES #10.

DC Comics
1700 Broadway, New York, NY 10019
A Warner Bros. Entertainment Company

Cataloging-in-Publication Data is available at the Library of Congress website:
ISBN: 978-1-4342-6479-4 (library binding)

Summary: Superman's old foe General Zod has escaped from the Phantom Zone--to open up a hot dog stand! Can Superman save Metropolis from the fiery footsteps of fifty-foot frankfurters? Maybe--but can he finish his lunch first?

STONE ARCH BOOKS
Ashley C. Andersen Zantop Publisher
Michael Dahl Editorial Director
Donald Lemke & Sean Tulien Editors
Brann Garvey & Russell Griesmer Designers
Kathy McColley Production Specialist

DC COMICS
Kristy Quinn Original U.S. Editor

Printed in China by Nordica.
1013/CA21301918
092013 007744NORDS14

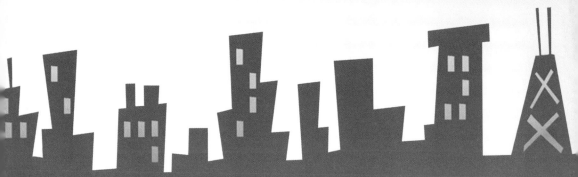

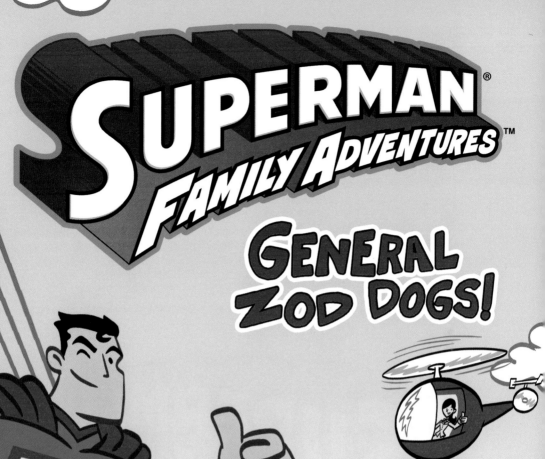

SUPERMAN® FAMILY ADVENTURES™

GENERAL ZOD DOGS!

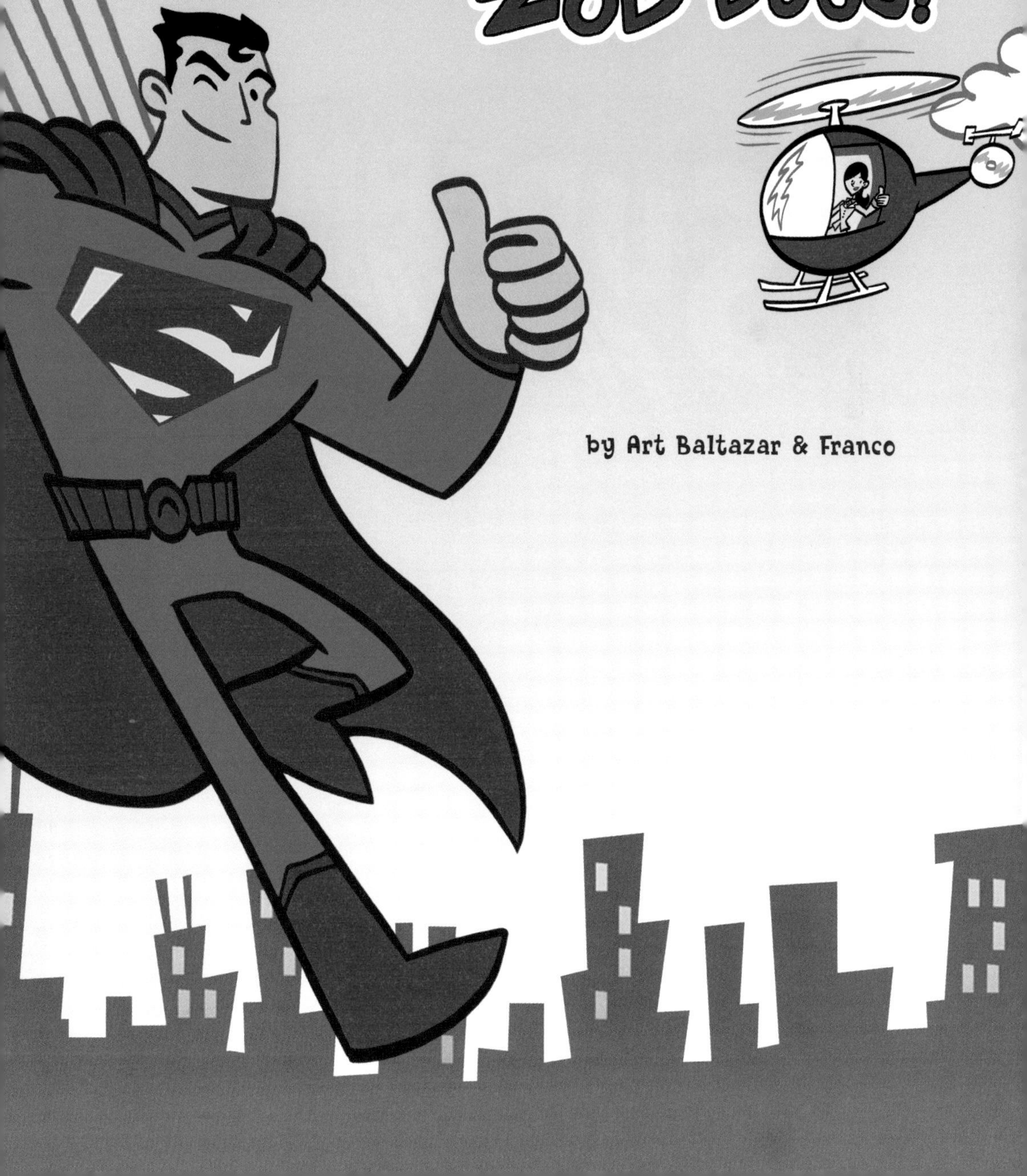

by Art Baltazar & Franco

SUPERMAN
FAMILY ADVENTURES

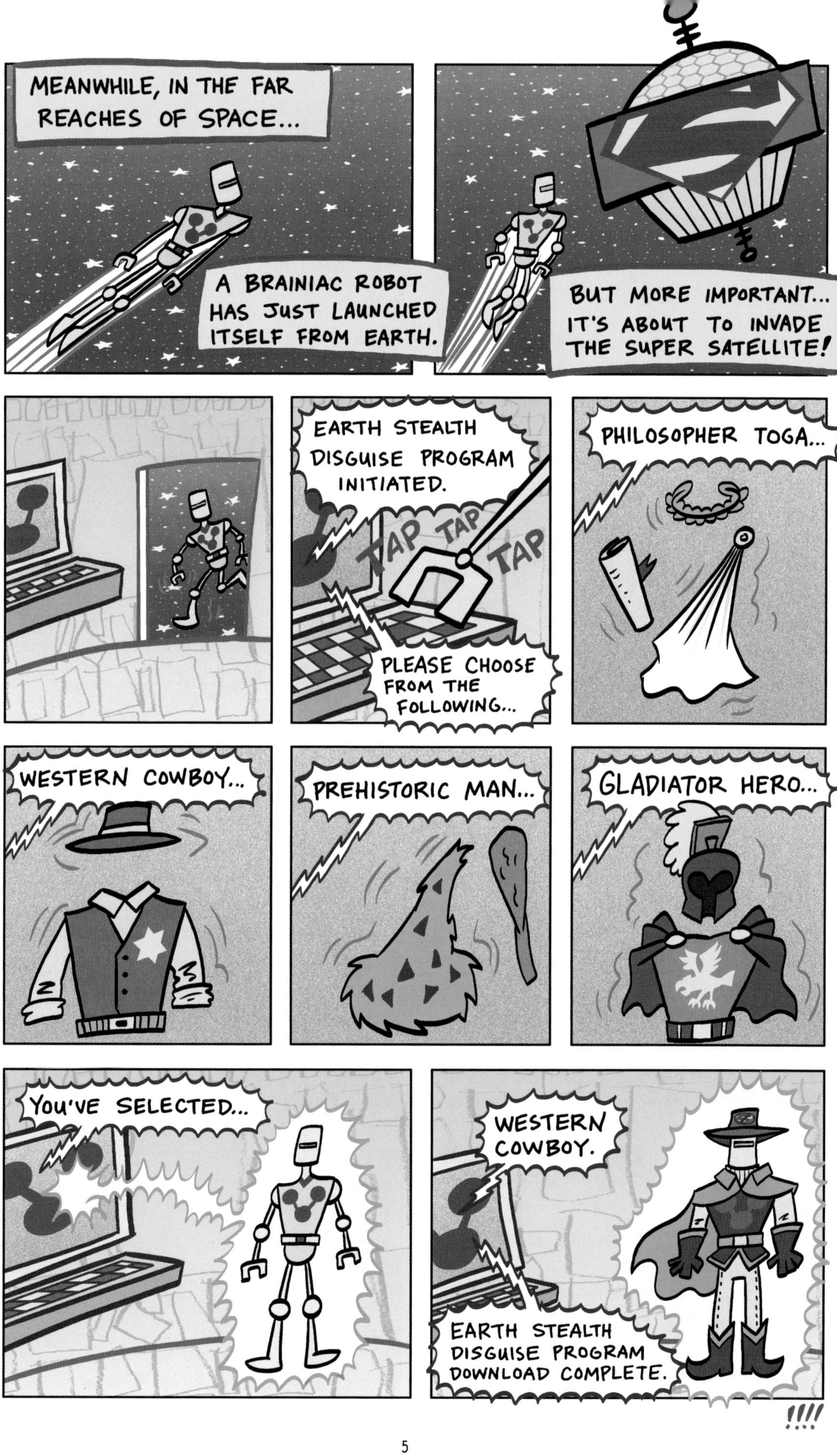
MEANWHILE, IN THE FAR REACHES OF SPACE...
A BRAINIAC ROBOT HAS JUST LAUNCHED ITSELF FROM EARTH.
BUT MORE IMPORTANT... IT'S ABOUT TO INVADE THE SUPER SATELLITE!
EARTH STEALTH DISGUISE PROGRAM INITIATED.
TAP TAP TAP
PLEASE CHOOSE FROM THE FOLLOWING...
PHILOSOPHER TOGA...
WESTERN COWBOY...
PREHISTORIC MAN...
GLADIATOR HERO...
YOU'VE SELECTED...
WESTERN COWBOY.
EARTH STEALTH DISGUISE PROGRAM DOWNLOAD COMPLETE.
!!!!

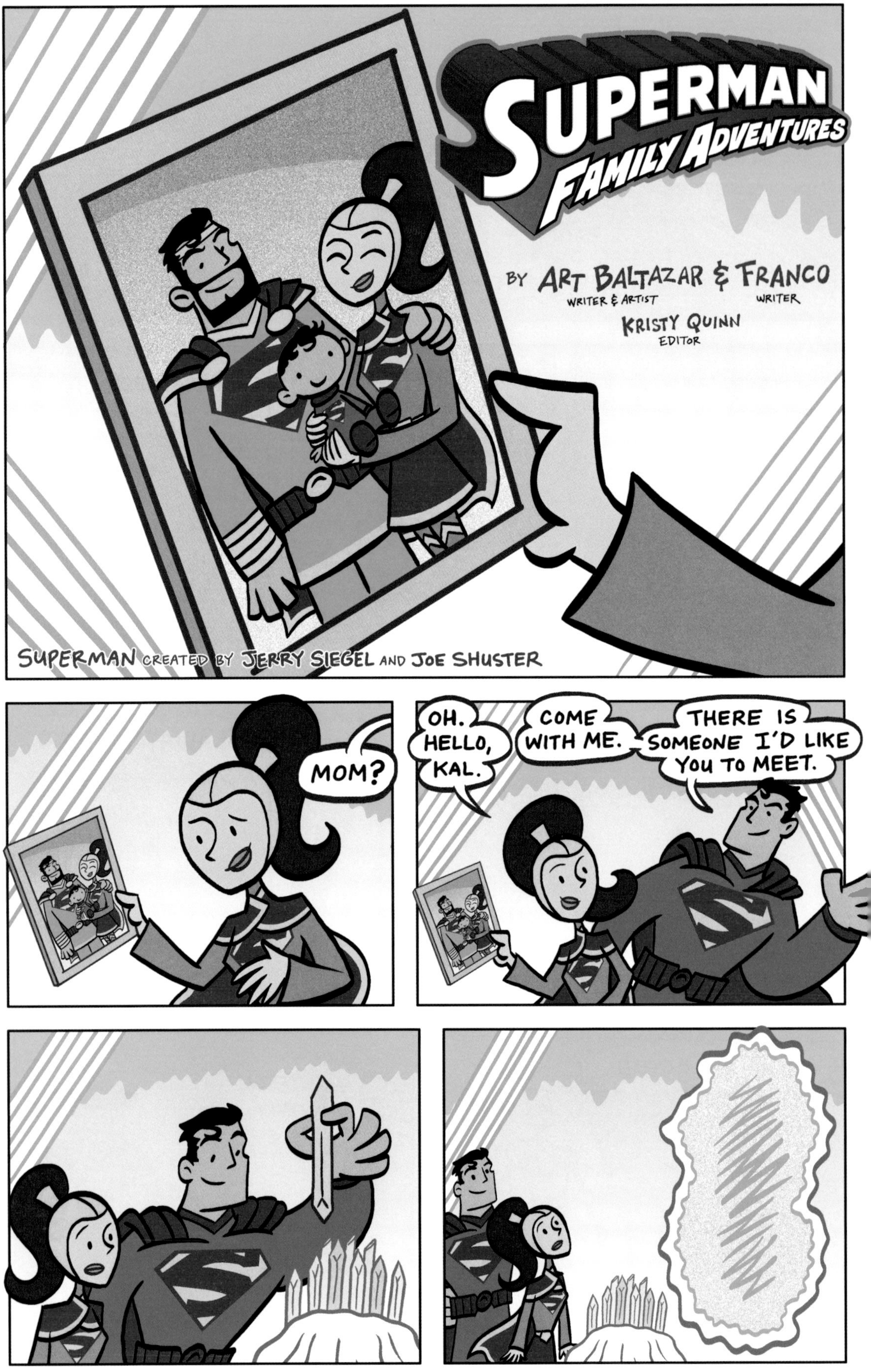
SUPERMAN FAMILY ADVENTURES
BY ART BALTAZAR & FRANCO
WRITER & ARTIST
WRITER
KRISTY QUINN
EDITOR
SUPERMAN CREATED BY JERRY SIEGEL AND JOE SHUSTER
MOM?
OH. HELLO, KAL.
COME WITH ME.
THERE IS SOMEONE I'D LIKE YOU TO MEET.

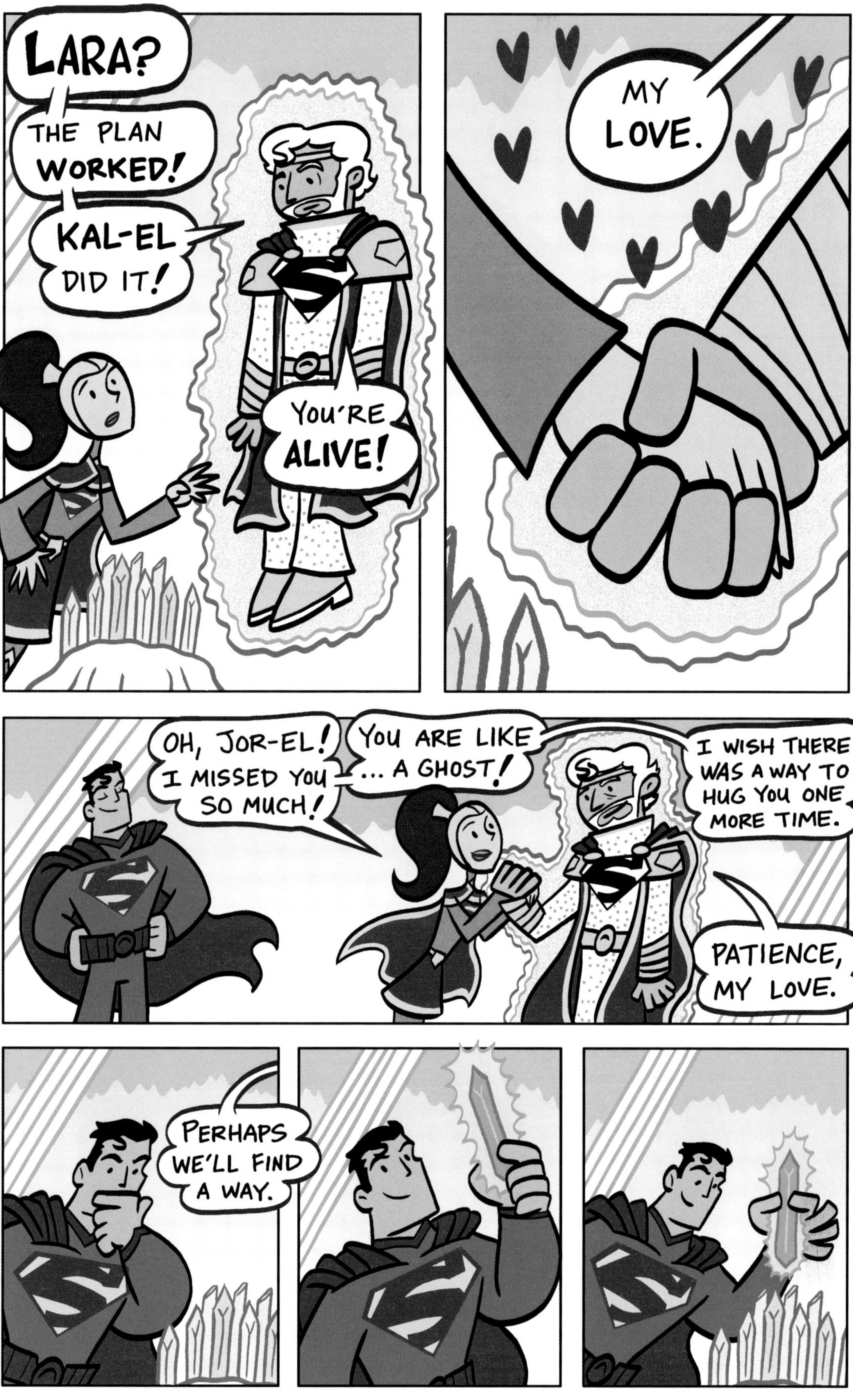
LARA?
THE PLAN WORKED!
KAL-EL DID IT!
YOU'RE ALIVE!
MY LOVE.
OH, JOR-EL! I MISSED YOU SO MUCH!
YOU ARE LIKE ... A GHOST!
I WISH THERE WAS A WAY TO HUG YOU ONE MORE TIME.
PATIENCE, MY LOVE.
PERHAPS WE'LL FIND A WAY.

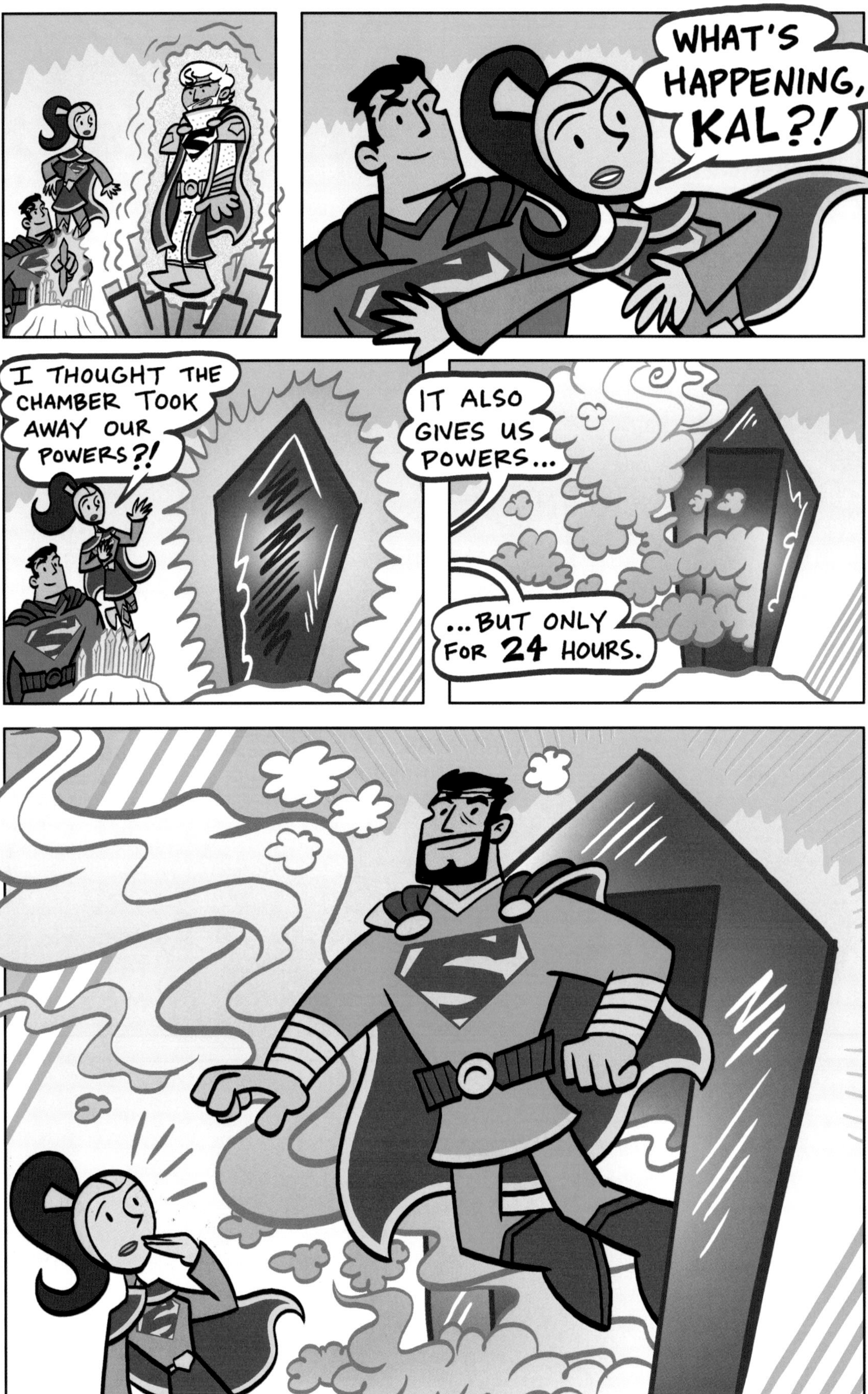
WHAT'S HAPPENING, KAL?!
I THOUGHT THE CHAMBER TOOK AWAY OUR POWERS?!
IT ALSO GIVES US POWERS...
...BUT ONLY FOR 24 HOURS.

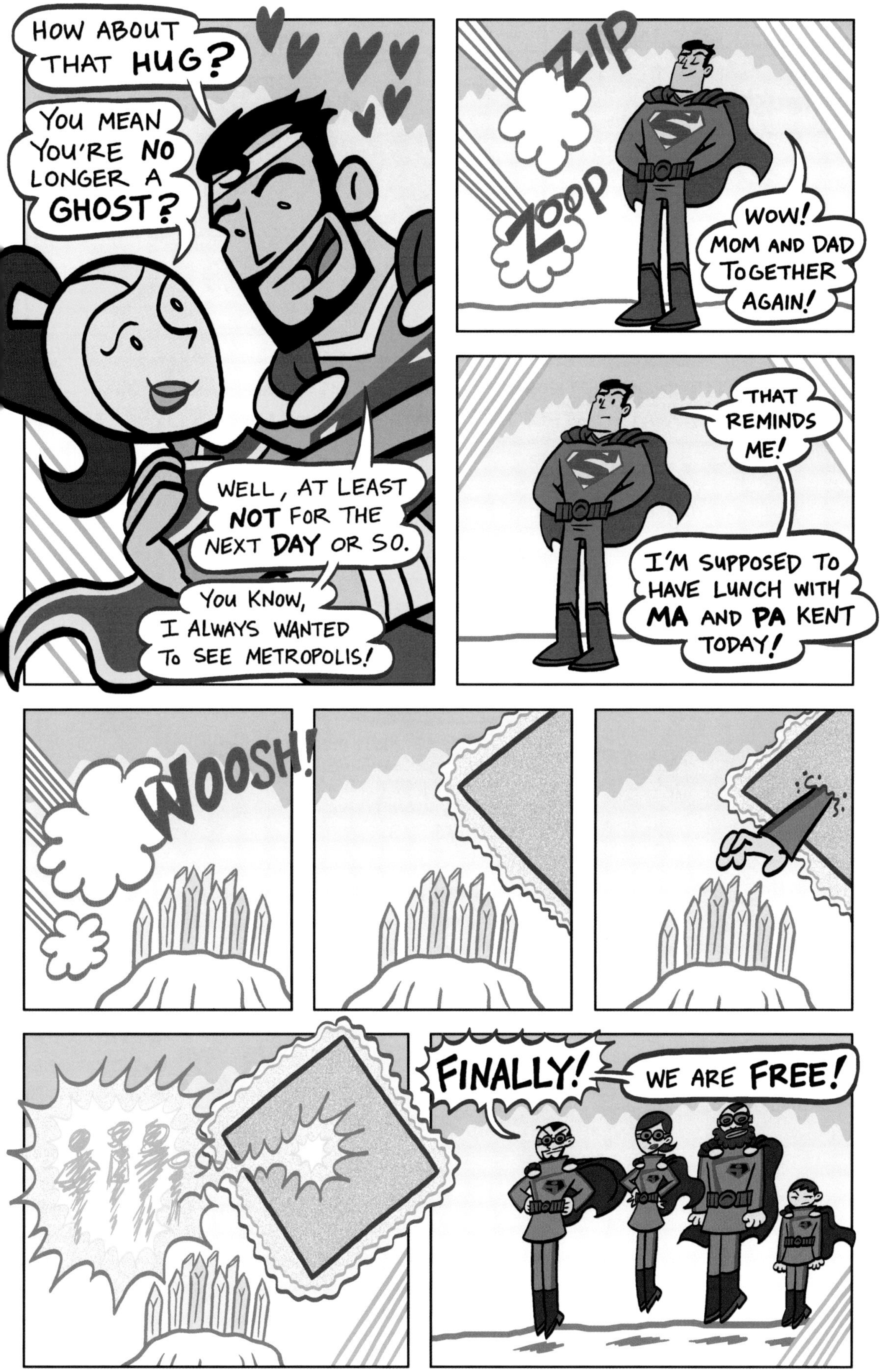
HOW ABOUT THAT HUG?
YOU MEAN YOU'RE NO LONGER A GHOST?
WELL, AT LEAST NOT FOR THE NEXT DAY OR SO.
YOU KNOW, I ALWAYS WANTED TO SEE METROPOLIS!
ZIP
ZOOP
WOW! MOM AND DAD TOGETHER AGAIN!
THAT REMINDS ME!
I'M SUPPOSED TO HAVE LUNCH WITH MA AND PA KENT TODAY!
WOOSH!
FINALLY!
WE ARE FREE!

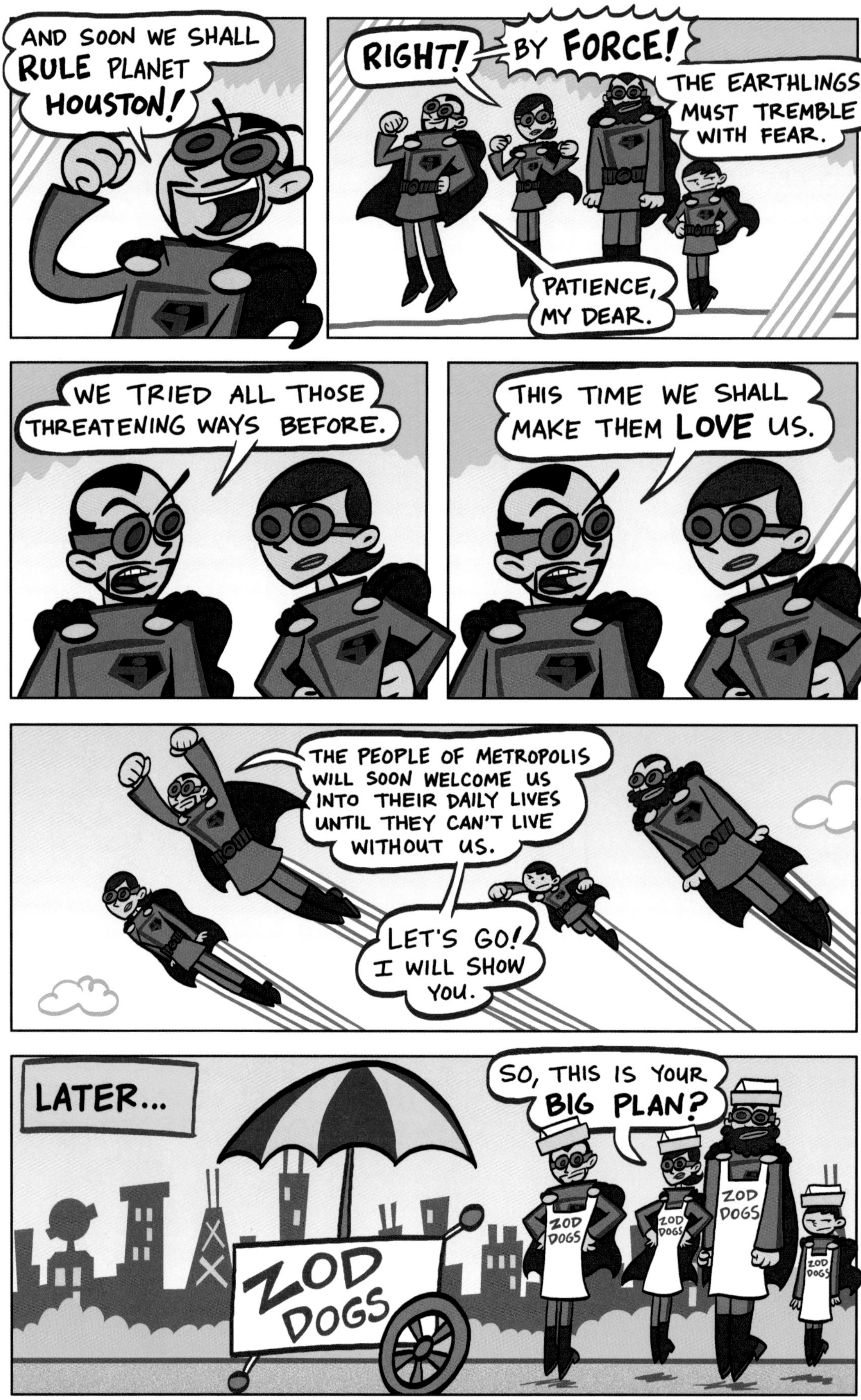

AND SOON WE SHALL RULE PLANET HOUSTON!
RIGHT!
BY FORCE!
THE EARTHLINGS MUST TREMBLE WITH FEAR.
PATIENCE, MY DEAR.
WE TRIED ALL THOSE THREATENING WAYS BEFORE.
THIS TIME WE SHALL MAKE THEM LOVE US.
THE PEOPLE OF METROPOLIS WILL SOON WELCOME US INTO THEIR DAILY LIVES UNTIL THEY CAN'T LIVE WITHOUT US.
LET'S GO! I WILL SHOW YOU.
LATER...
ZOD DOGS
SO, THIS IS YOUR BIG PLAN?
ZOD DOGS
ZOD DOGS
ZOD DOGS
ZOD DOGS

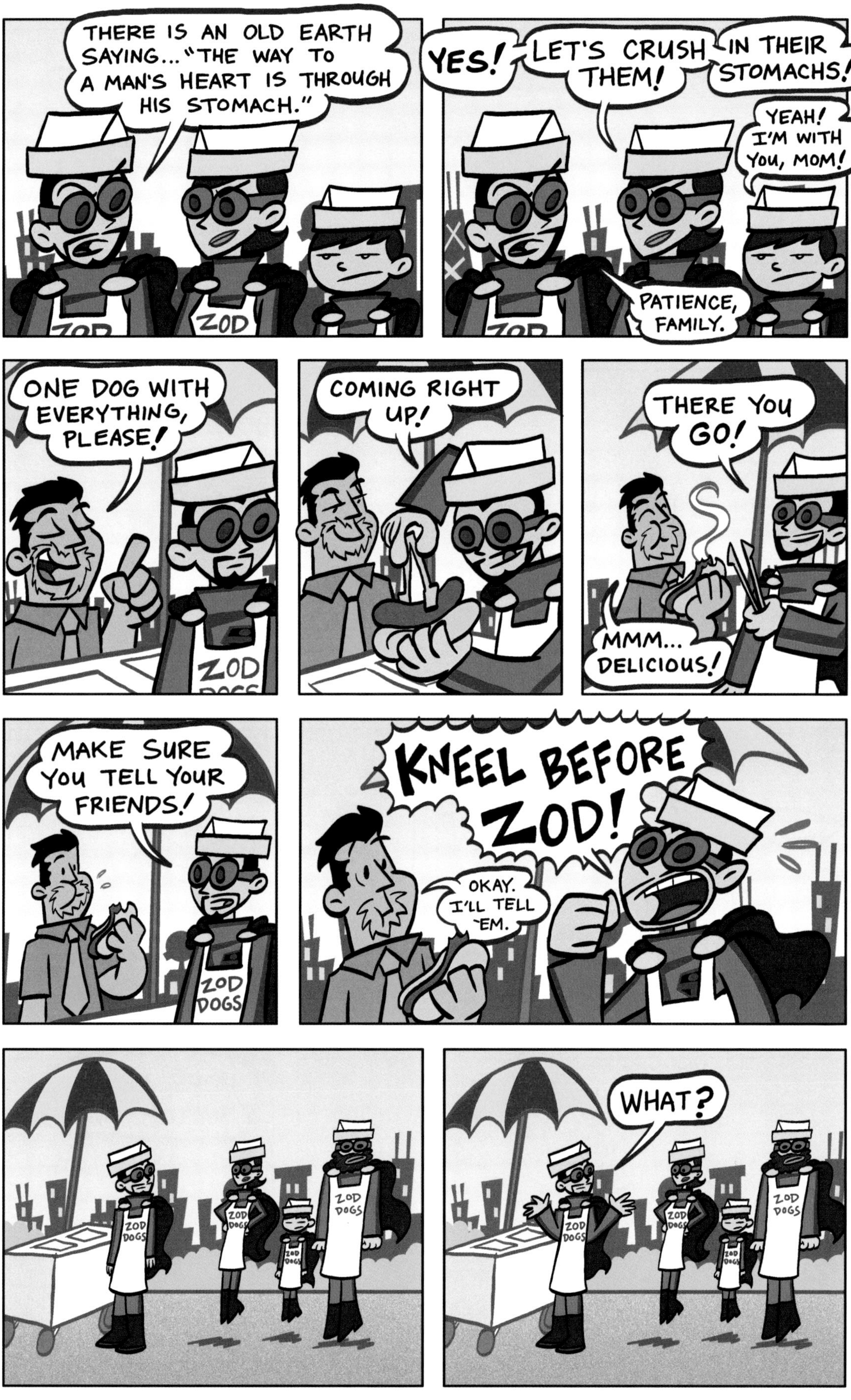
THERE IS AN OLD EARTH SAYING... "THE WAY TO A MAN'S HEART IS THROUGH HIS STOMACH."
ZOD
ZOD
YES!
LET'S CRUSH THEM!
IN THEIR STOMACHS!
YEAH! I'M WITH YOU, MOM!
PATIENCE, FAMILY.
ONE DOG WITH EVERYTHING, PLEASE!
ZOD
COMING RIGHT UP!
THERE YOU GO!
MMM... DELICIOUS!
MAKE SURE YOU TELL YOUR FRIENDS!
ZOD DOGS
KNEEL BEFORE ZOD!
OKAY. I'LL TELL 'EM.
ZOD DOGS
ZOD DOGS
ZOD DOGS
ZOD DOGS
WHAT?
ZOD DOGS
ZOD DOGS
ZOD DOGS
ZOD DOGS

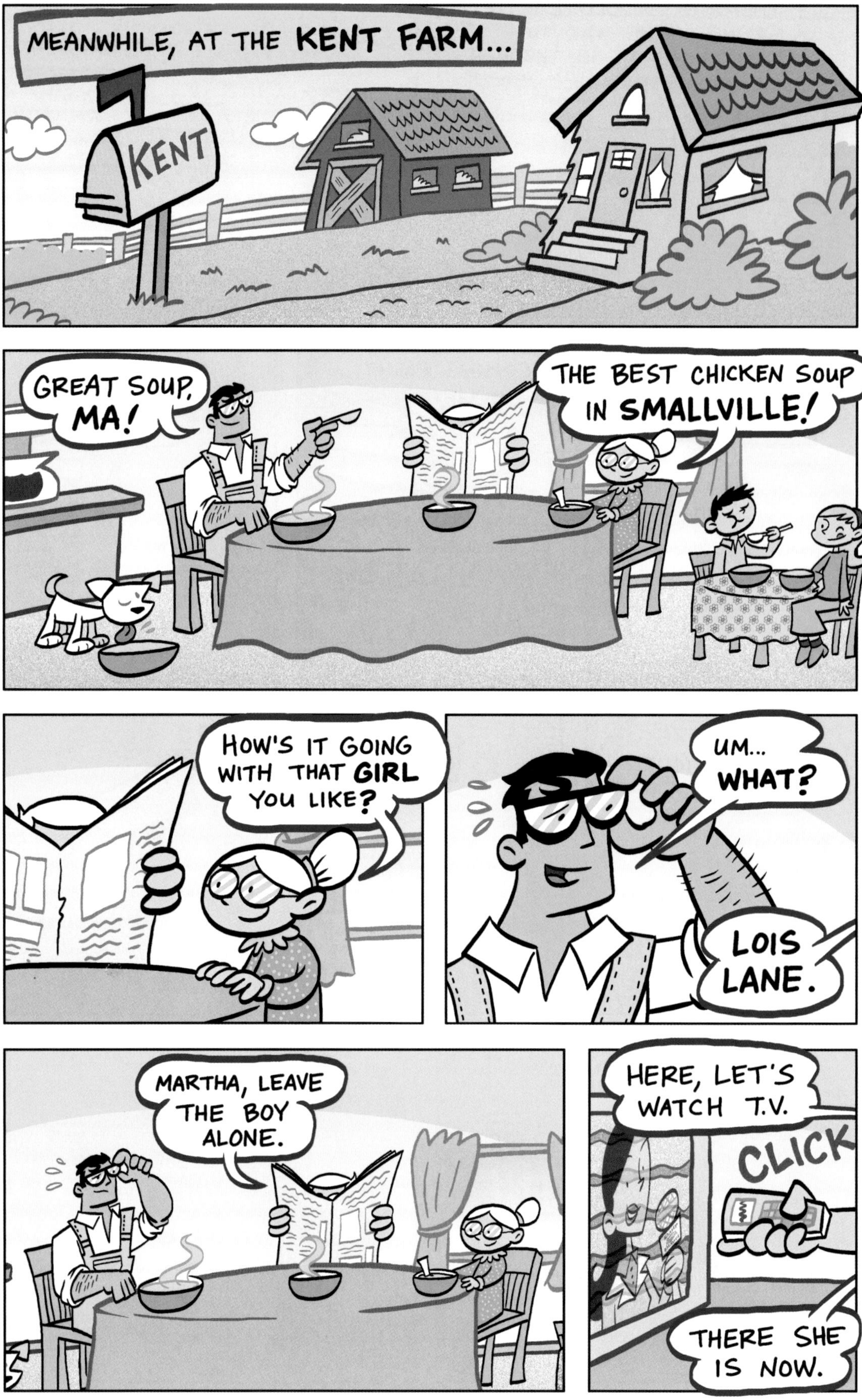
MEANWHILE, AT THE KENT FARM...
KENT
GREAT SOUP, MA!
THE BEST CHICKEN SOUP IN SMALLVILLE!
HOW'S IT GOING WITH THAT GIRL YOU LIKE?
UM... WHAT?
LOIS LANE.
MARTHA, LEAVE THE BOY ALONE.
HERE, LET'S WATCH T.V.
CLICK
THERE SHE IS NOW.

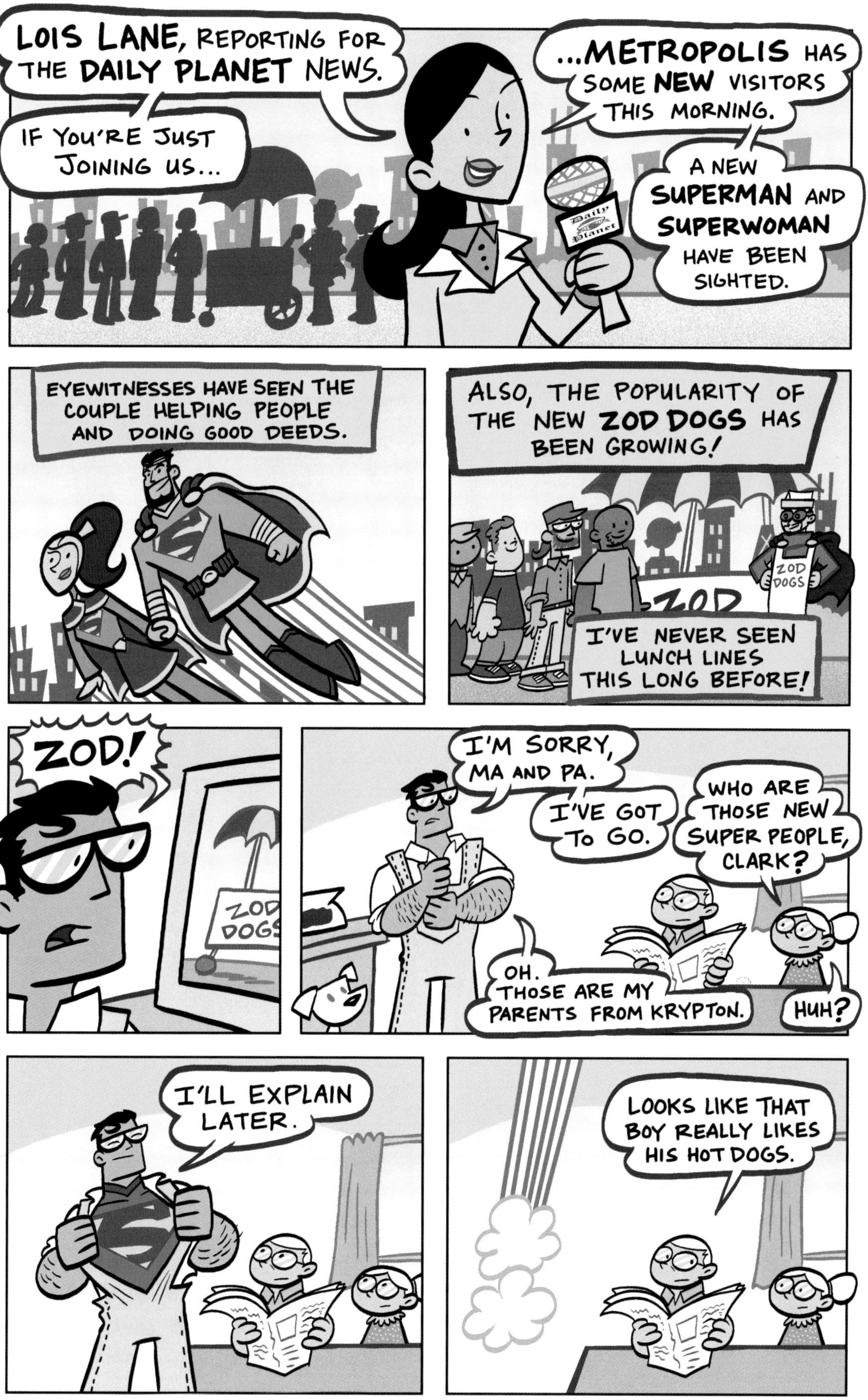
LOIS LANE, REPORTING FOR THE DAILY PLANET NEWS.
IF YOU'RE JUST JOINING US...
...METROPOLIS HAS SOME NEW VISITORS THIS MORNING.
A NEW SUPERMAN AND SUPERWOMAN HAVE BEEN SIGHTED.
Daily Planet
EYEWITNESSES HAVE SEEN THE COUPLE HELPING PEOPLE AND DOING GOOD DEEDS.
ALSO, THE POPULARITY OF THE NEW ZOD DOGS HAS BEEN GROWING!
ZOD DOGS
I'VE NEVER SEEN LUNCH LINES THIS LONG BEFORE!
ZOD!
I'M SORRY, MA AND PA.
I'VE GOT TO GO.
WHO ARE THOSE NEW SUPER PEOPLE, CLARK?
OH. THOSE ARE MY PARENTS FROM KRYPTON.
HUH?
I'LL EXPLAIN LATER.
LOOKS LIKE THAT BOY REALLY LIKES HIS HOT DOGS.

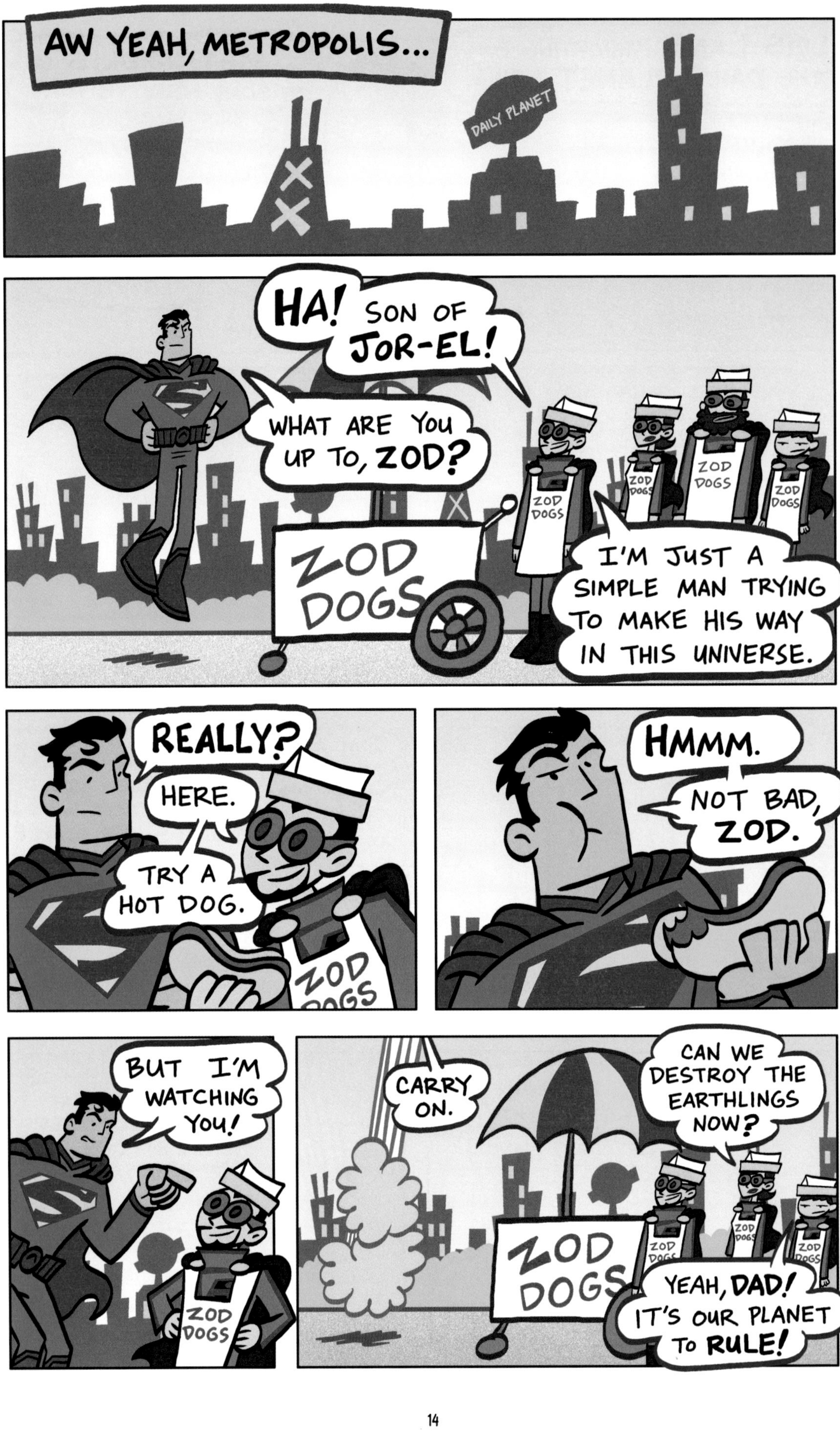
AW YEAH, METROPOLIS...
DAILY PLANET
HA! SON OF JOR-EL!
WHAT ARE YOU UP TO, ZOD?
ZOD DOGS
I'M JUST A SIMPLE MAN TRYING TO MAKE HIS WAY IN THIS UNIVERSE.
REALLY?
HERE.
TRY A HOT DOG.
HMMM.
NOT BAD, ZOD.
BUT I'M WATCHING YOU!
CARRY ON.
CAN WE DESTROY THE EARTHLINGS NOW?
YEAH, DAD! IT'S OUR PLANET TO RULE!

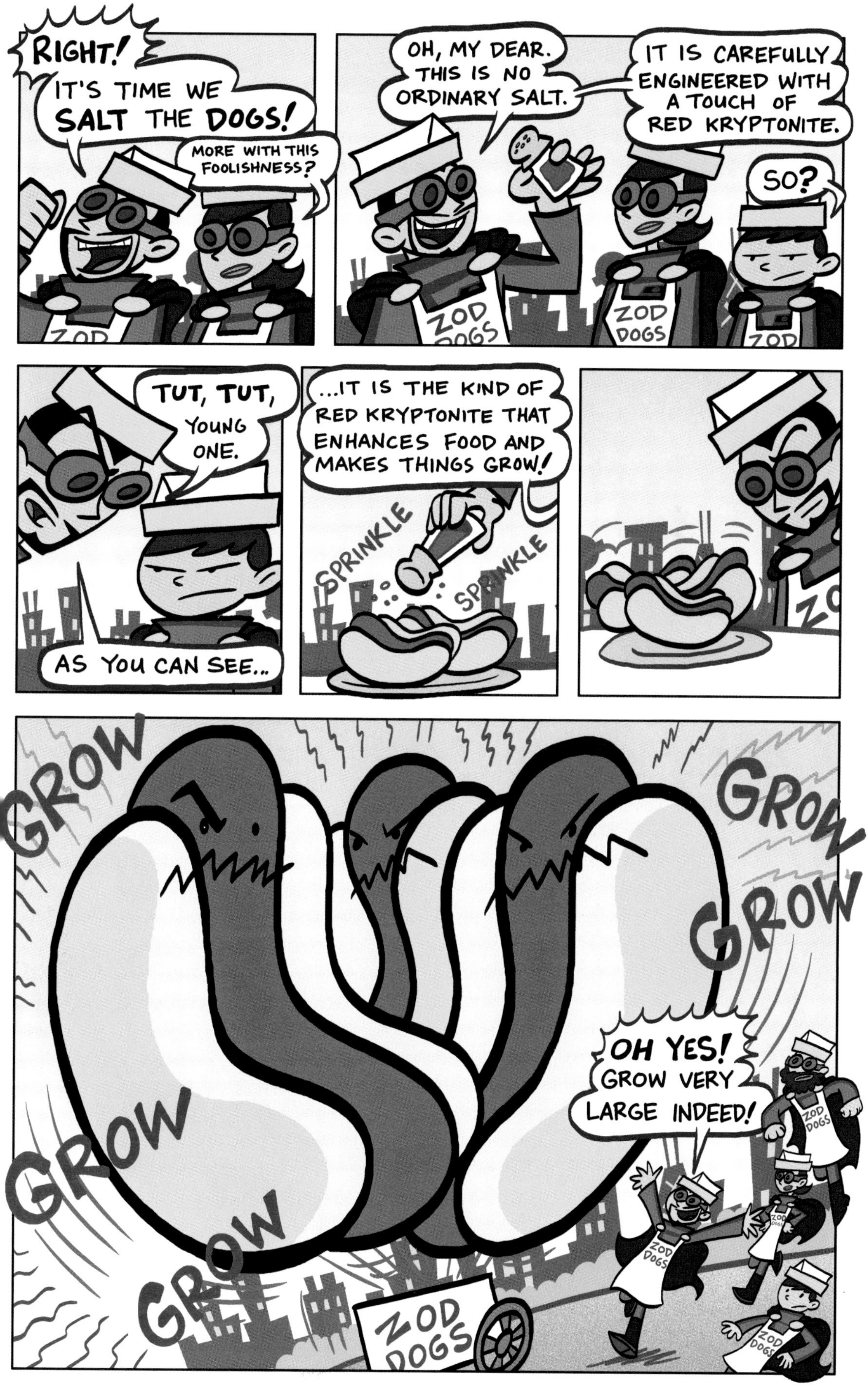
RIGHT!
IT'S TIME WE SALT THE DOGS!
MORE WITH THIS FOOLISHNESS?
OH, MY DEAR. THIS IS NO ORDINARY SALT.
IT IS CAREFULLY ENGINEERED WITH A TOUCH OF RED KRYPTONITE.
SO?
ZOD DOGS
ZOD DOGS
TUT, TUT, YOUNG ONE.
AS YOU CAN SEE...
...IT IS THE KIND OF RED KRYPTONITE THAT ENHANCES FOOD AND MAKES THINGS GROW!
SPRINKLE
SPRINKLE
GROW
GROW
GROW
GROW
GROW
GROW
OH YES! GROW VERY LARGE INDEED!
ZOD DOGS
ZOD DOGS
ZOD DOGS
ZOD DOGS
ZOD DOGS

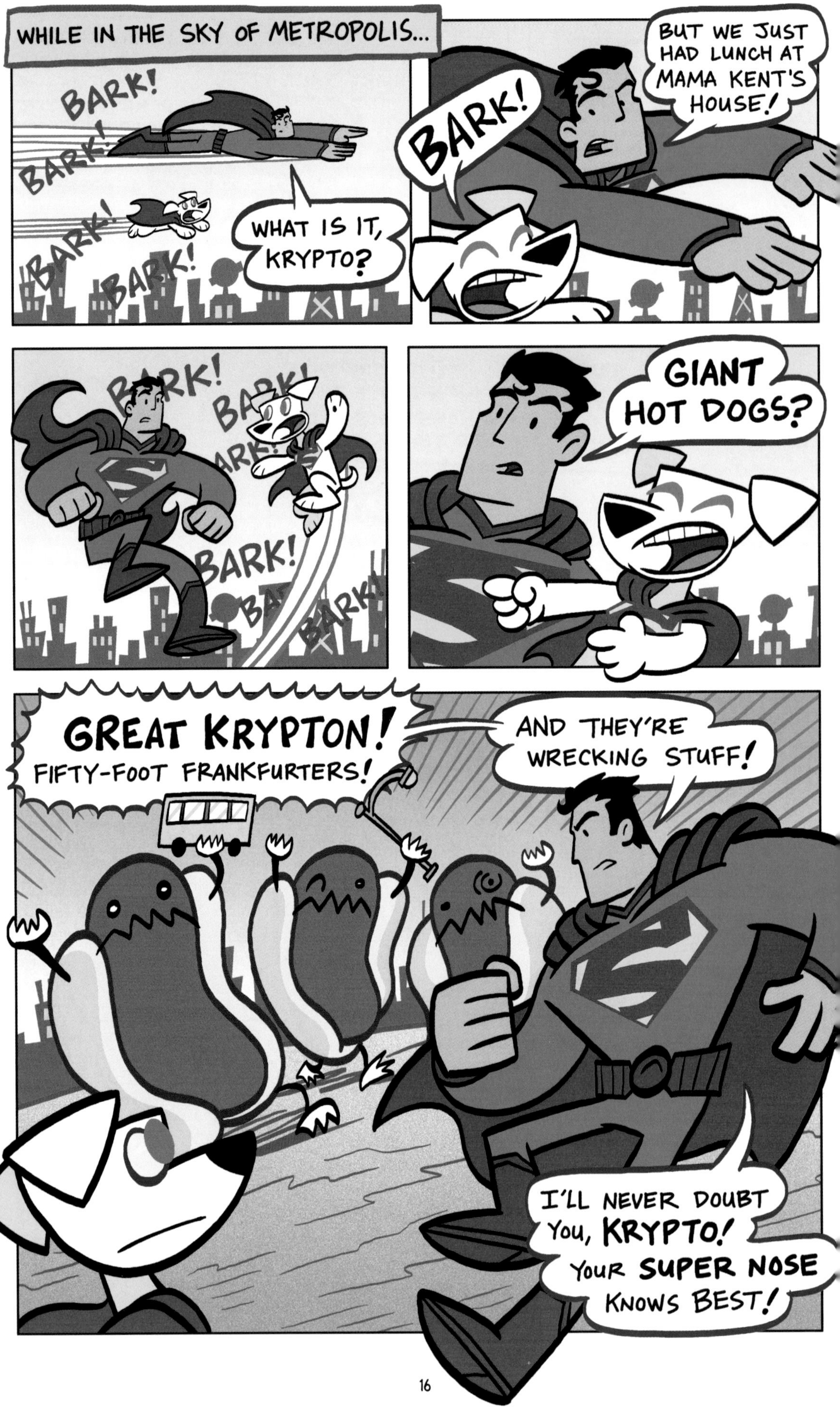
WHILE IN THE SKY OF METROPOLIS...
BARK!
BARK!
BARK!
BARK!
WHAT IS IT, KRYPTO?
BARK!
BUT WE JUST HAD LUNCH AT MAMA KENT'S HOUSE!
BARK!
BARK!
GIANT HOT DOGS?
GREAT KRYPTON! FIFTY-FOOT FRANKFURTERS!
AND THEY'RE WRECKING STUFF!
I'LL NEVER DOUBT YOU, KRYPTO! YOUR SUPER NOSE KNOWS BEST!

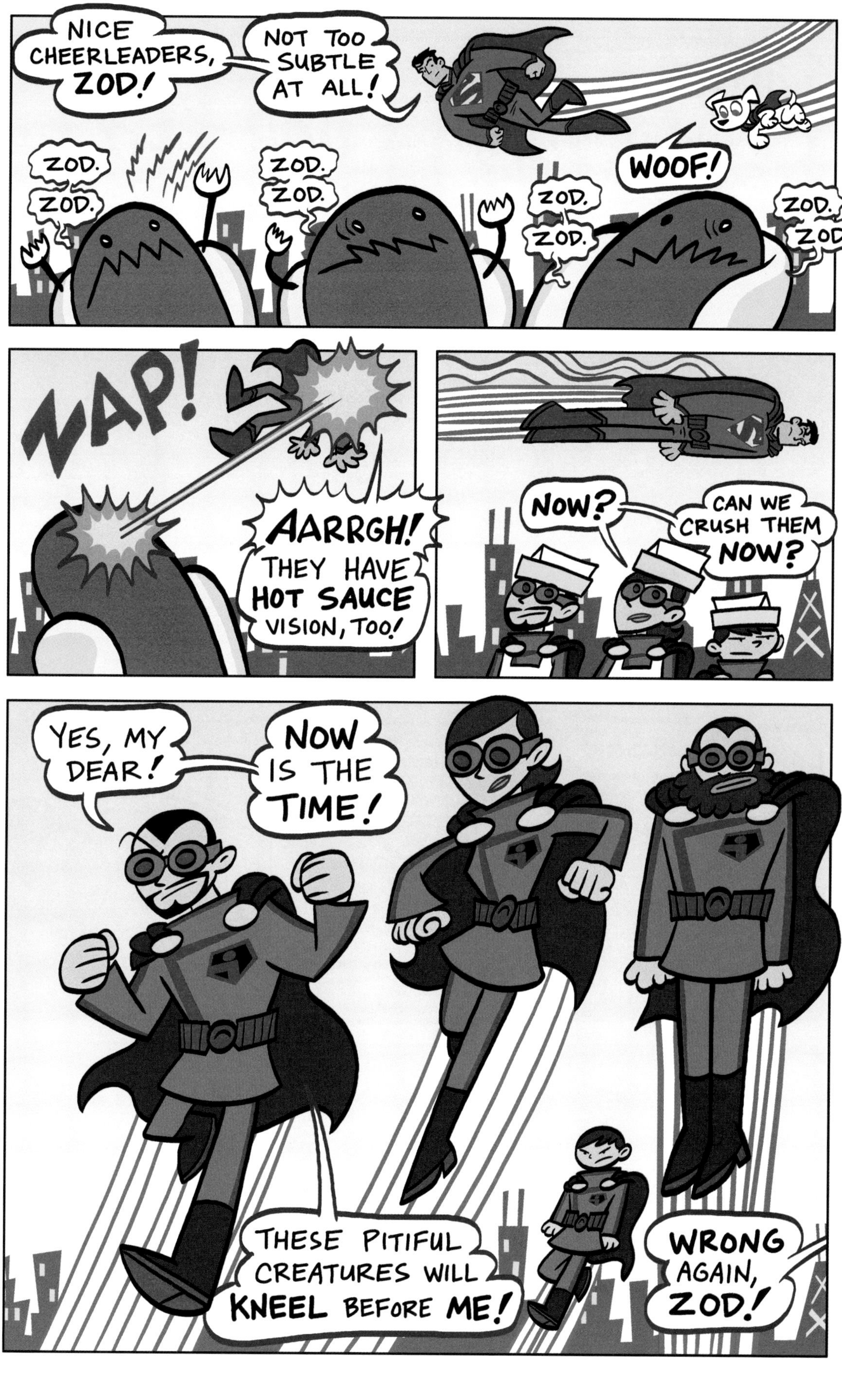
NICE CHEERLEADERS, ZOD!
NOT TOO SUBTLE AT ALL!
ZOD. ZOD.
ZOD. ZOD.
ZOD. ZOD.
WOOF!
ZOD. ZOD.
ZAP!
AARRGH! THEY HAVE HOT SAUCE VISION, TOO!
NOW?
CAN WE CRUSH THEM NOW?
YES, MY DEAR!
NOW IS THE TIME!
THESE PITIFUL CREATURES WILL KNEEL BEFORE ME!
WRONG AGAIN, ZOD!

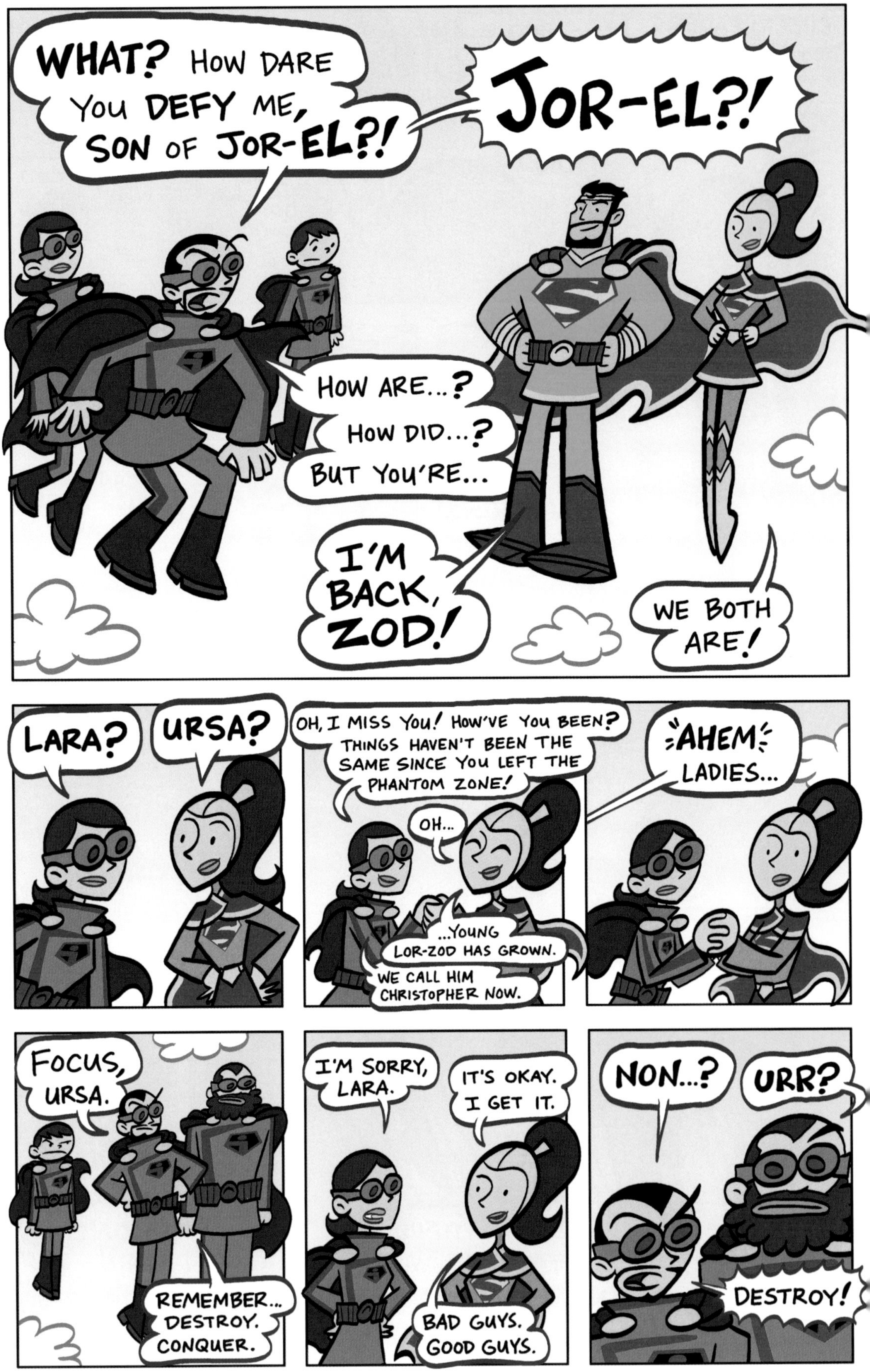
WHAT? HOW DARE YOU DEFY ME, SON OF JOR-EL?!
JOR-EL?!
HOW ARE...?
HOW DID...?
BUT YOU'RE...
I'M BACK, ZOD!
WE BOTH ARE!
LARA?
URSA?
OH, I MISS YOU! HOW'VE YOU BEEN? THINGS HAVEN'T BEEN THE SAME SINCE YOU LEFT THE PHANTOM ZONE!
OH...
...YOUNG LOR-ZOD HAS GROWN.
WE CALL HIM CHRISTOPHER NOW.
AHEM LADIES...
FOCUS, URSA.
REMEMBER... DESTROY. CONQUER.
I'M SORRY, LARA.
IT'S OKAY. I GET IT.
BAD GUYS. GOOD GUYS.
NON...?
URR?
DESTROY!

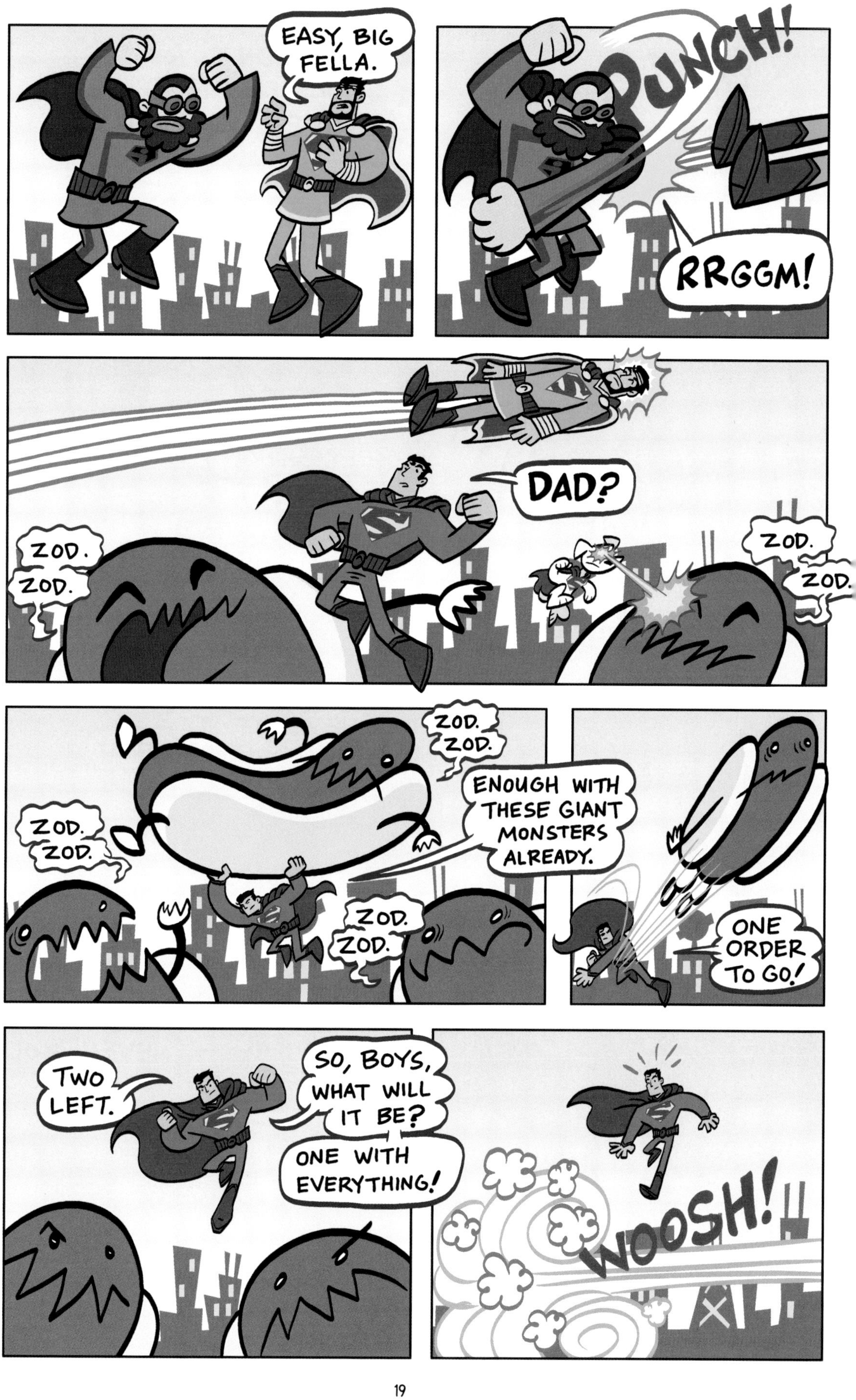
EASY, BIG FELLA.
PUNCH!
RRGGM!
DAD?
ZOD.
ZOD.
ZOD.
ZOD.
ZOD.
ZOD.
ZOD.
ZOD.
ENOUGH WITH THESE GIANT MONSTERS ALREADY.
ZOD.
ZOD.
ONE ORDER TO GO!
TWO LEFT.
SO, BOYS, WHAT WILL IT BE?
ONE WITH EVERYTHING!
WOOSH!

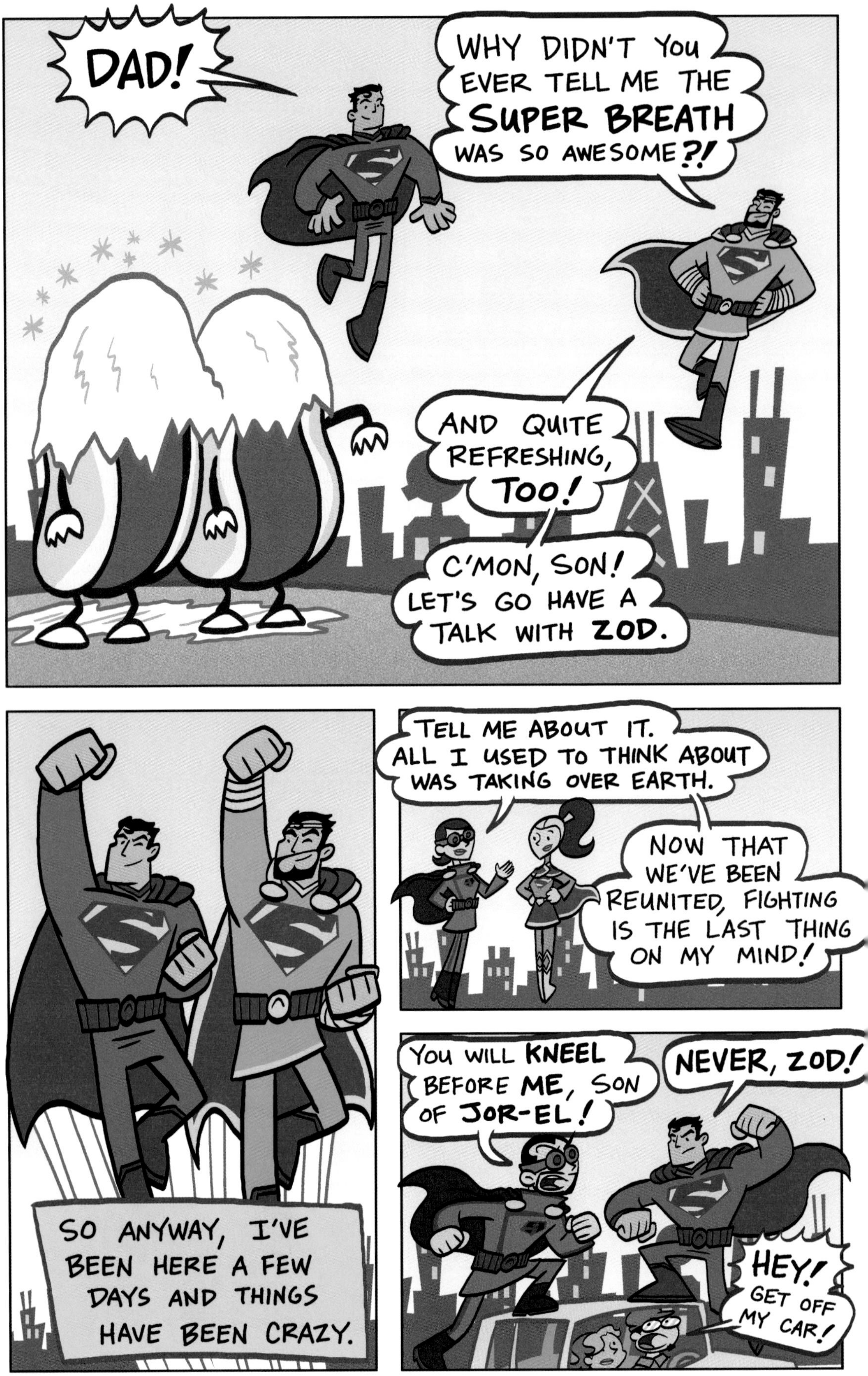

DAD!
WHY DIDN'T YOU EVER TELL ME THE SUPER BREATH WAS SO AWESOME?!
AND QUITE REFRESHING, TOO!
C'MON, SON! LET'S GO HAVE A TALK WITH ZOD.
SO ANYWAY, I'VE BEEN HERE A FEW DAYS AND THINGS HAVE BEEN CRAZY.
TELL ME ABOUT IT. ALL I USED TO THINK ABOUT WAS TAKING OVER EARTH.
NOW THAT WE'VE BEEN REUNITED, FIGHTING IS THE LAST THING ON MY MIND!
YOU WILL KNEEL BEFORE ME, SON OF JOR-EL!
NEVER, ZOD!
HEY! GET OFF MY CAR!

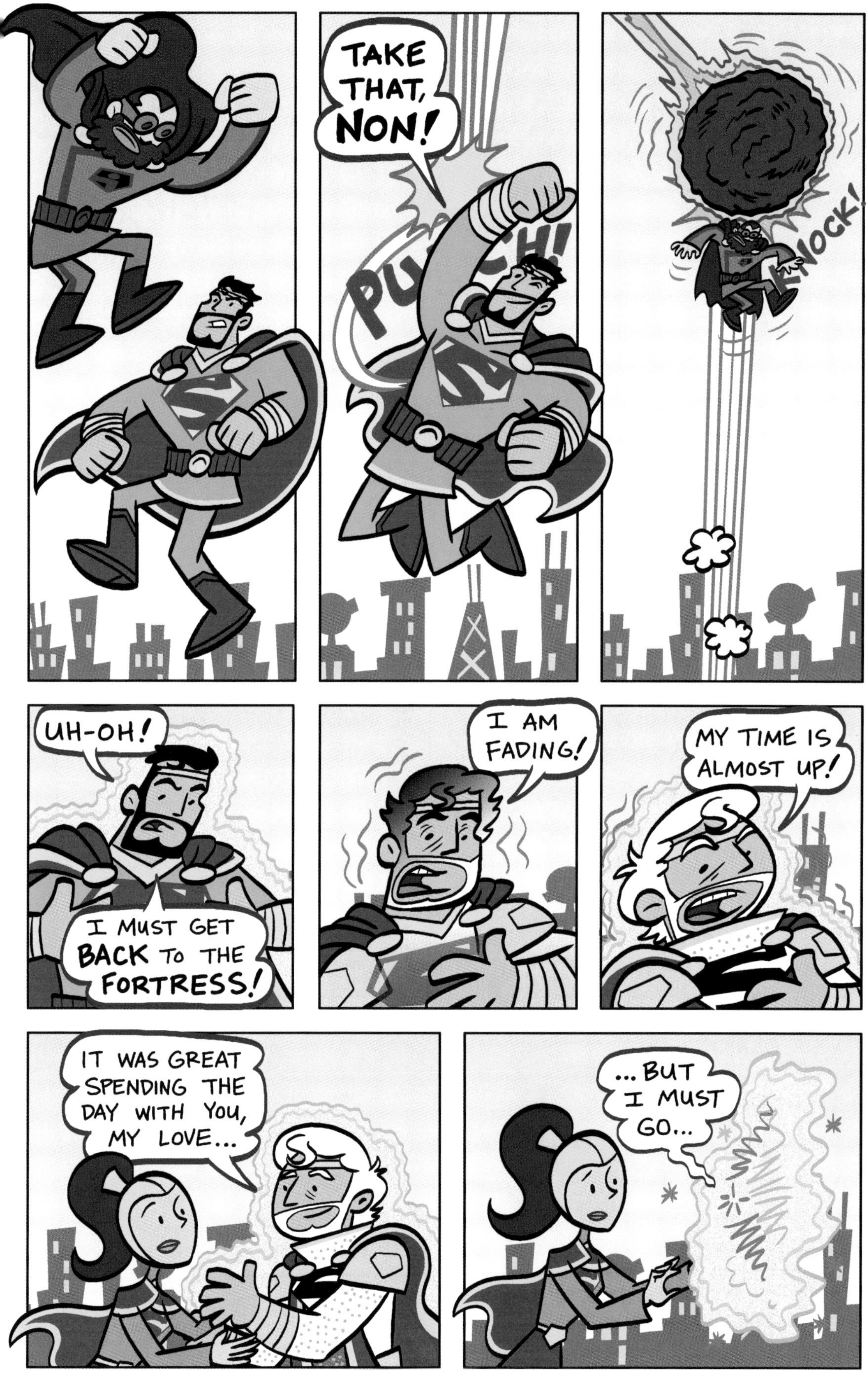
TAKE THAT, NON!
PUNCH!
KNOCK!
UH-OH!
I MUST GET BACK TO THE FORTRESS!
I AM FADING!
MY TIME IS ALMOST UP!
IT WAS GREAT SPENDING THE DAY WITH YOU, MY LOVE...
...BUT I MUST GO...

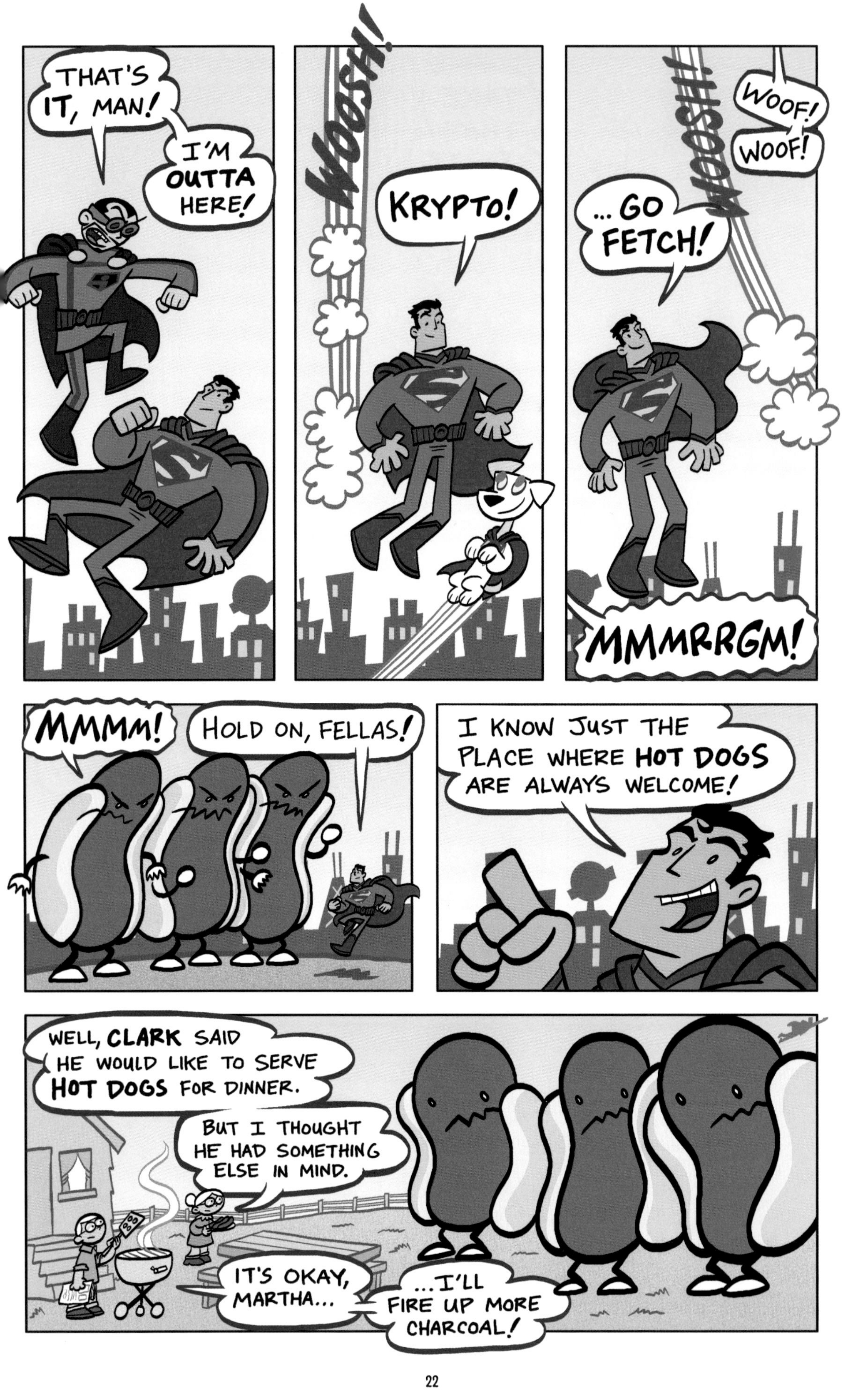

THAT'S IT, MAN!
I'M OUTTA HERE!
WOOSH!
KRYPTO!
WOOSH!
WOOF! WOOF!
...GO FETCH!
MMMRRGM!
MMMM!
HOLD ON, FELLAS!
I KNOW JUST THE PLACE WHERE HOT DOGS ARE ALWAYS WELCOME!
WELL, CLARK SAID HE WOULD LIKE TO SERVE HOT DOGS FOR DINNER.
BUT I THOUGHT HE HAD SOMETHING ELSE IN MIND.
IT'S OKAY, MARTHA...
...I'LL FIRE UP MORE CHARCOAL!

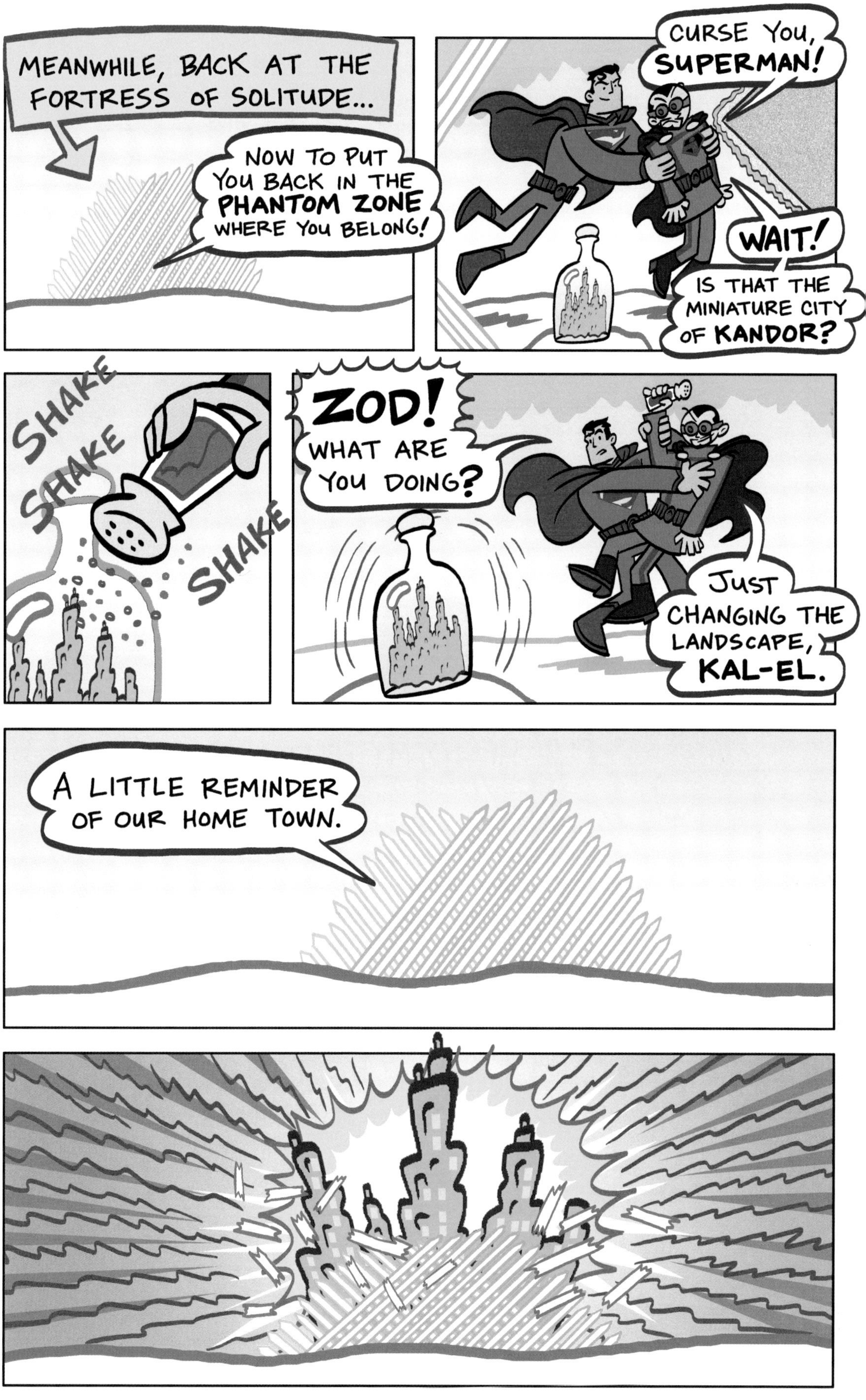
MEANWHILE, BACK AT THE FORTRESS OF SOLITUDE...
NOW TO PUT YOU BACK IN THE PHANTOM ZONE WHERE YOU BELONG!
CURSE YOU, SUPERMAN!
WAIT! IS THAT THE MINIATURE CITY OF KANDOR?
SHAKE
SHAKE
SHAKE
ZOD! WHAT ARE YOU DOING?
JUST CHANGING THE LANDSCAPE, KAL-EL.
A LITTLE REMINDER OF OUR HOME TOWN.

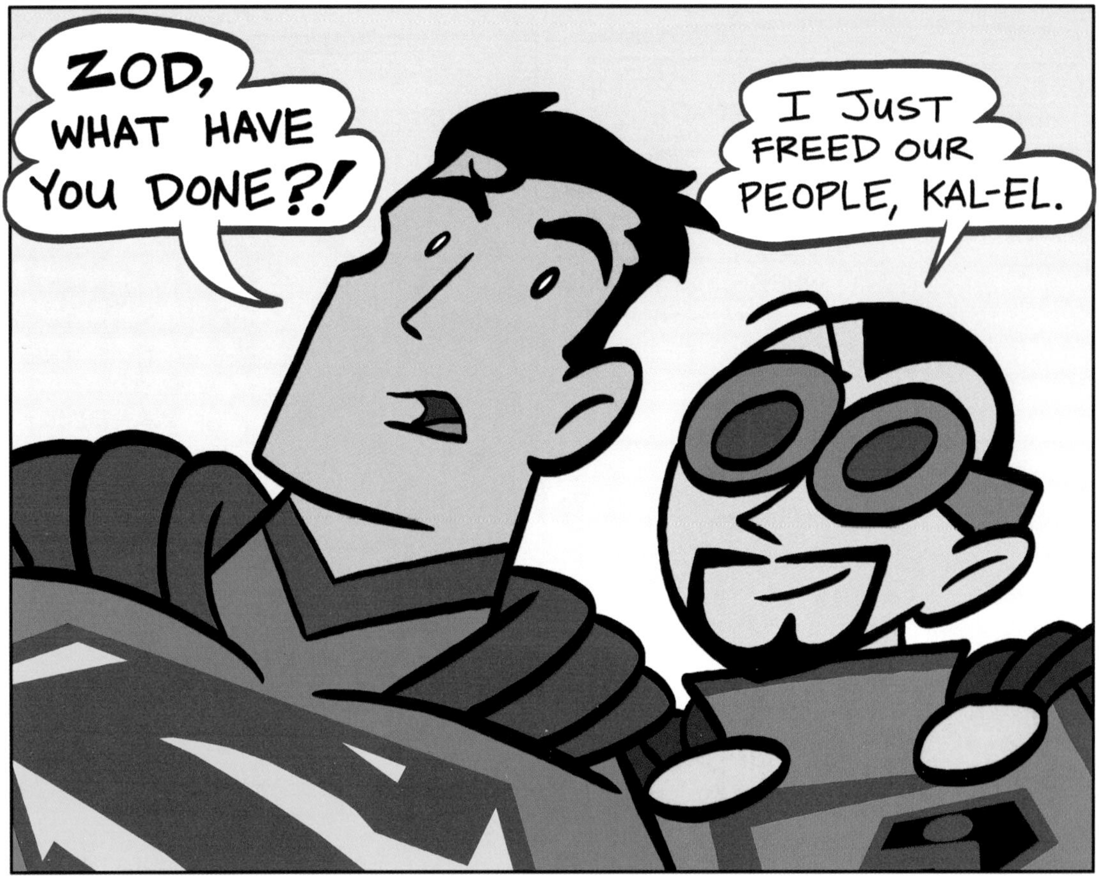
ZOD, WHAT HAVE YOU DONE?!
I JUST FREED OUR PEOPLE, KAL-EL.

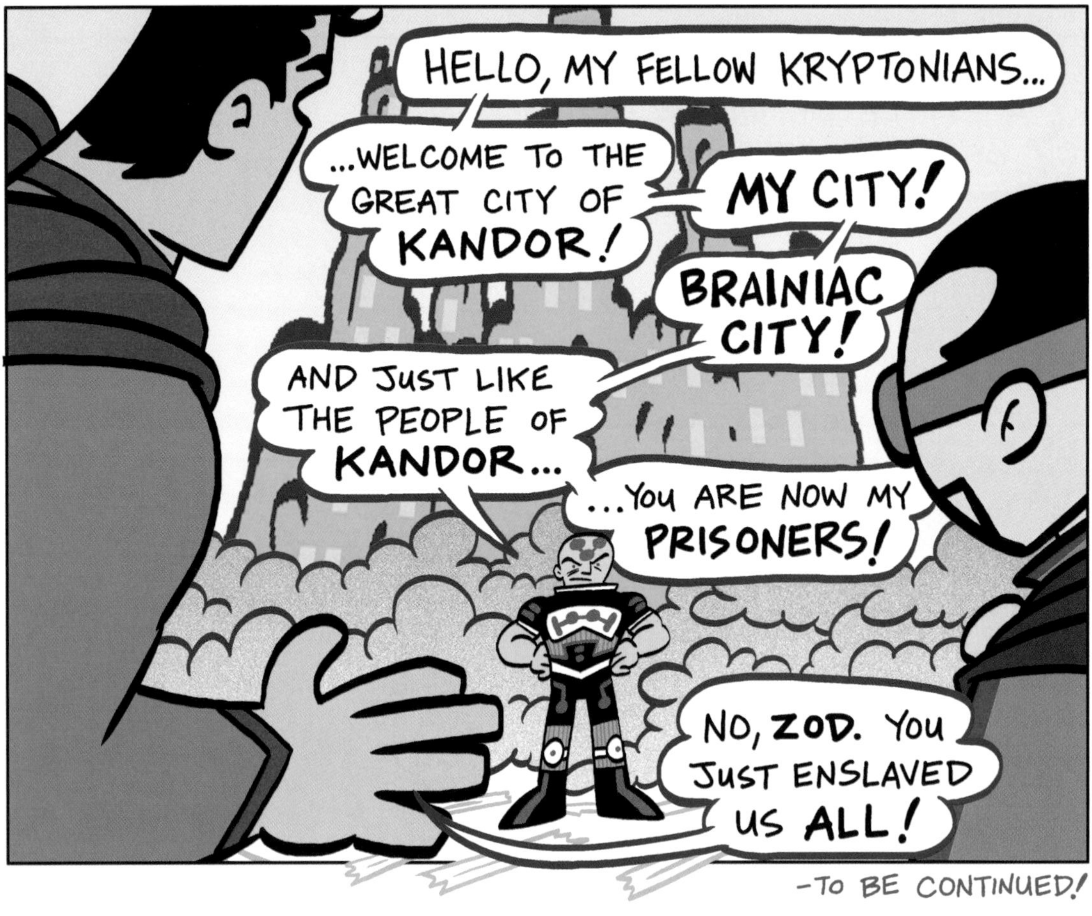
HELLO, MY FELLOW KRYPTONIANS...
...WELCOME TO THE GREAT CITY OF KANDOR!
MY CITY!
BRAINIAC CITY!
AND JUST LIKE THE PEOPLE OF KANDOR...
...YOU ARE NOW MY PRISONERS!
NO, ZOD. YOU JUST ENSLAVED US ALL!

–TO BE CONTINUED!

SUPERMAN®
FAMILY ADVENTURES™

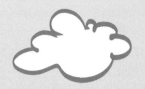

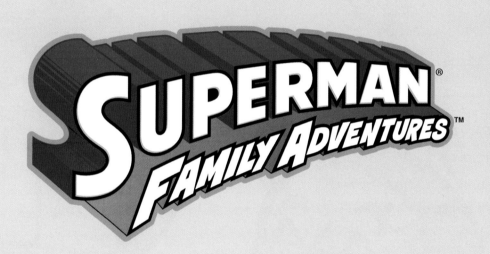

CREATORS

ART BALTAZAR IS A CARTOONIST MACHINE FROM THE HEART OF CHICAGO! HE DEFINES CARTOONS AND COMICS NOT ONLY AS AN ART STYLE, BUT AS A WAY OF LIFE. CURRENTLY, ART IS THE CREATIVE FORCE BEHIND THE NEW YORK TIMES BEST-SELLING, EISNER AWARD-WINNING, DC COMICS SERIES TINY TITANS, AND THE CO-WRITER FOR BILLY BATSON AND THE MAGIC OF SHAZAM! AND CO-CREATOR OF SUPERMAN FAMILY ADVENTURES. ART IS LIVING THE DREAM! HE DRAWS COMICS AND NEVER HAS TO LEAVE THE HOUSE. HE LIVES WITH HIS LOVELY WIFE, ROSE, BIG BOY SONNY, LITTLE BOY GORDON, AND LITTLE GIRL AUDREY. RIGHT ON!

ART BALTAZAR

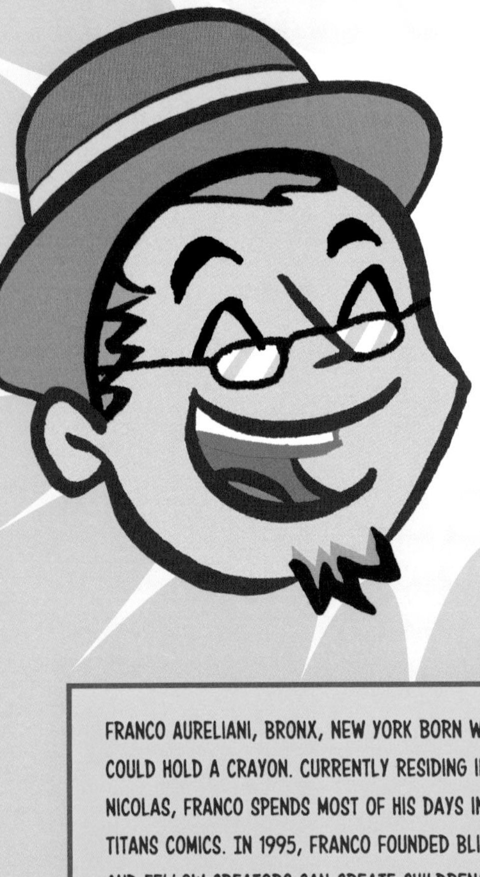

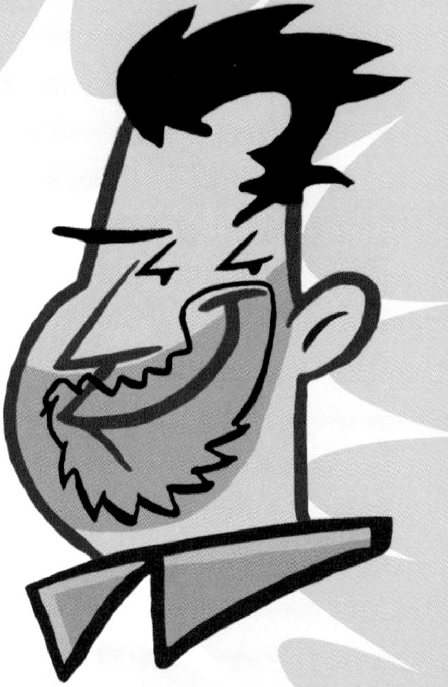

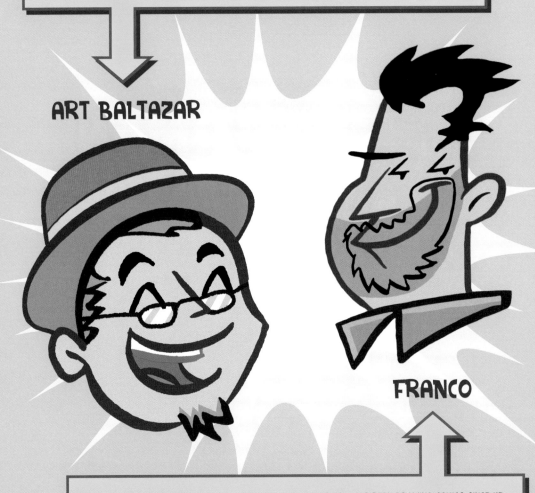

FRANCO

FRANCO AURELIANI, BRONX, NEW YORK BORN WRITER AND ARTIST, HAS BEEN DRAWING COMICS SINCE HE COULD HOLD A CRAYON. CURRENTLY RESIDING IN UPSTATE NEW YORK WITH HIS WIFE, IVETTE, AND SON, NICOLAS, FRANCO SPENDS MOST OF HIS DAYS IN A BATCAVE-LIKE STUDIO WHERE HE PRODUCES DC'S TINY TITANS COMICS. IN 1995, FRANCO FOUNDED BLINDWOLF STUDIOS, AN INDEPENDENT ART STUDIO WHERE HE AND FELLOW CREATORS CAN CREATE CHILDREN'S COMICS. FRANCO IS THE CREATOR, ARTIST, AND WRITER OF WEIRDSVILLE, L'IL CREEPS, AND EAGLE ALL STAR, AS WELL AS THE CO-CREATOR AND WRITER OF PATRICK THE WOLF BOY. WHEN HE'S NOT WRITING AND DRAWING, FRANCO ALSO TEACHES HIGH SCHOOL ART.

GLOSSARY

conquer (KONG-kur)—to defeat and take control of an enemy

defy (di-FYE)—refuse to obey

engineered (en-jun-NEERD)—made something happen by using a clever plan

enhance (en-HANSS)—to make something better or greater

enslaved (en-SLAVED)—made into a servant or slave

invade (in-VADE)—to send armed forces into another area in order to take it over

pitiful (PIT-i-fuhl)—useless or worthless

solitude (SOL-i-tood)—the state of being alone

stealth (STELTH)—if you do something stealthily, you do it secretly or sneakily

tremble (TREM-buhl)—shake or vibrate

VISUAL QUESTIONS & PROMPTS

1. BASED ON WHAT YOU KNOW ABOUT CLARK, HOW DO YOU THINK HE FEELS AFTER MA KENT ASKS HIM ABOUT LOIS? WHAT DO THE LITTLE DROPLETS OF WATER NEXT TO CLARK'S HEAD MEAN?

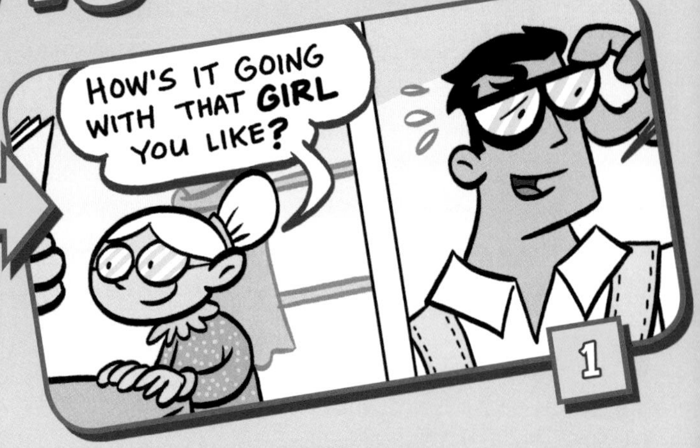
HOW'S IT GOING WITH THAT GIRL YOU LIKE?
1

2. THIS VILLAIN DECIDES ON A DISGUISE FOR INVADING EARTH. WHAT ARE SOME OTHER, MORE REALISTIC DISGUISES IT COULD HAVE CHOSEN?

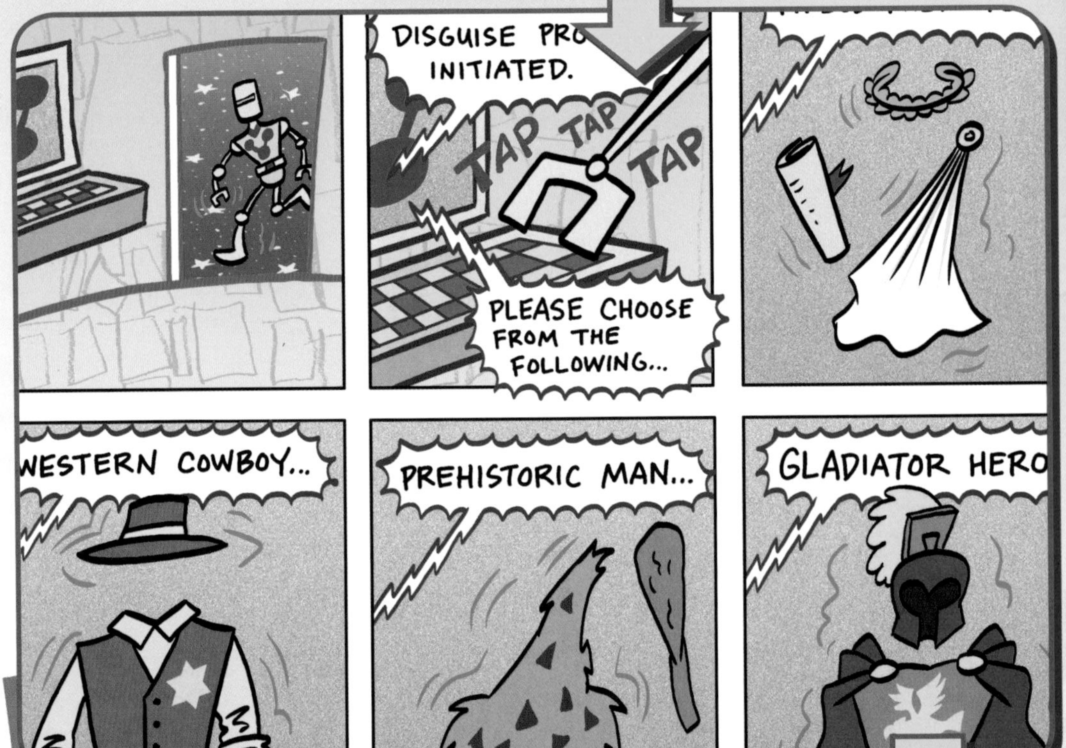
DISGUISE PRO
INITIATED.
TAP TAP TAP
PLEASE CHOOSE FROM THE FOLLOWING...
WESTERN COWBOY...
PREHISTORIC MAN...
GLADIATOR HERO
2

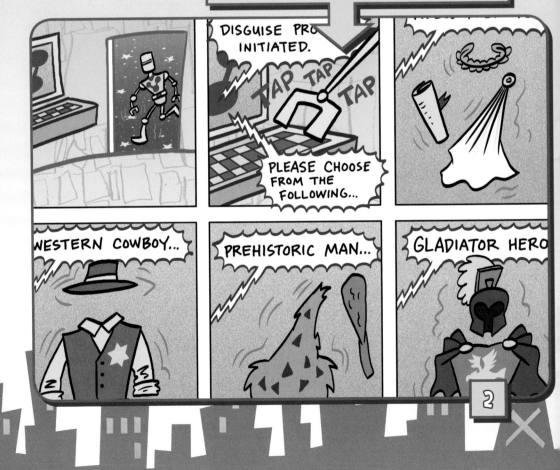

3. WHAT DO YOU THINK MA KENT MEANT WHEN SHE SAID "BUT I THOUGHT HE HAD SOMETHING ELSE IN MIND?"

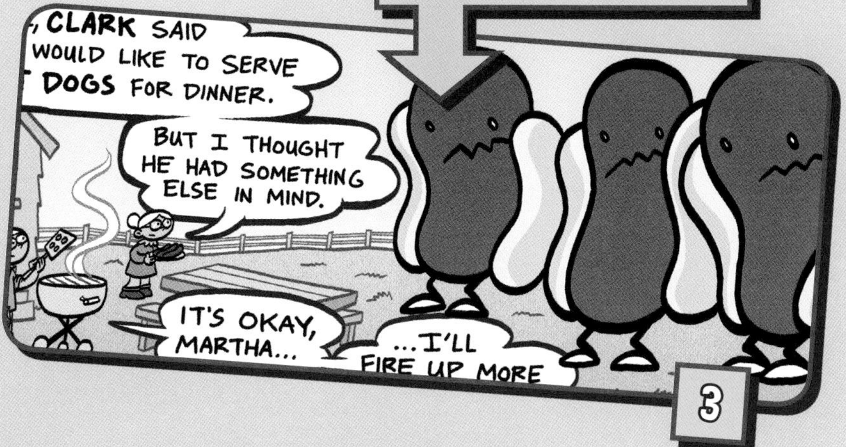

, CLARK SAID WOULD LIKE TO SERVE DOGS FOR DINNER.
BUT I THOUGHT HE HAD SOMETHING ELSE IN MIND.
IT'S OKAY, MARTHA...
...I'LL FIRE UP MORE
3

4. WHAT DO YOU THINK KRYPTO WAS TRYING TO TELL SUPERMAN WITH ALL HIS BARKING?

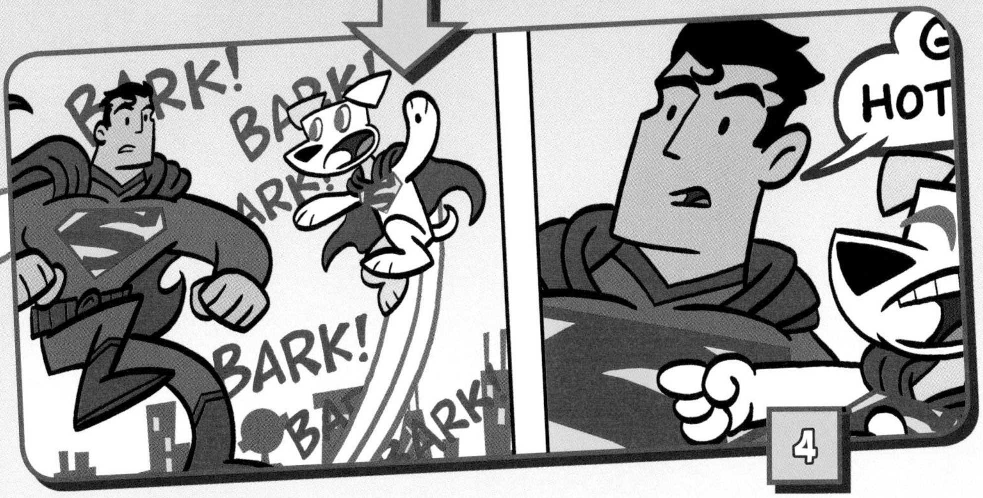

BARK!
BARK!
BARK!
HOT
4

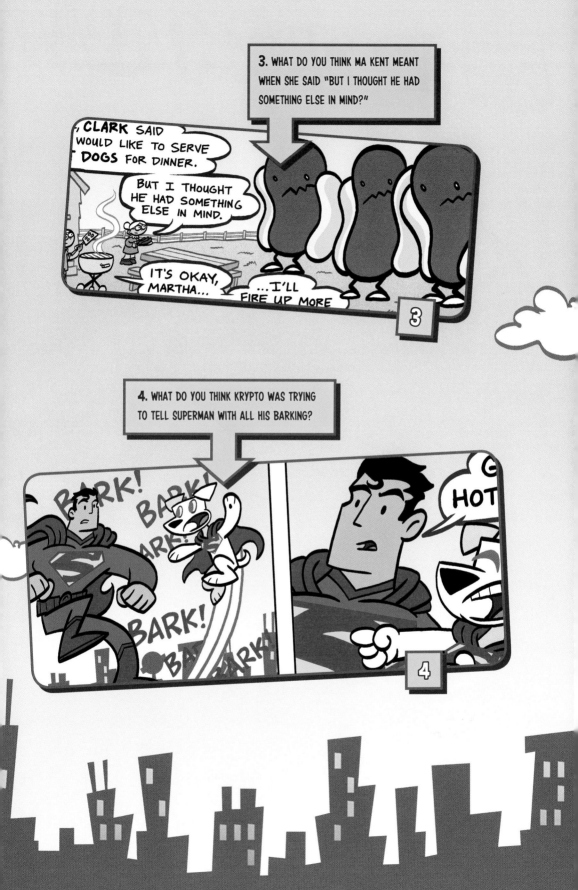

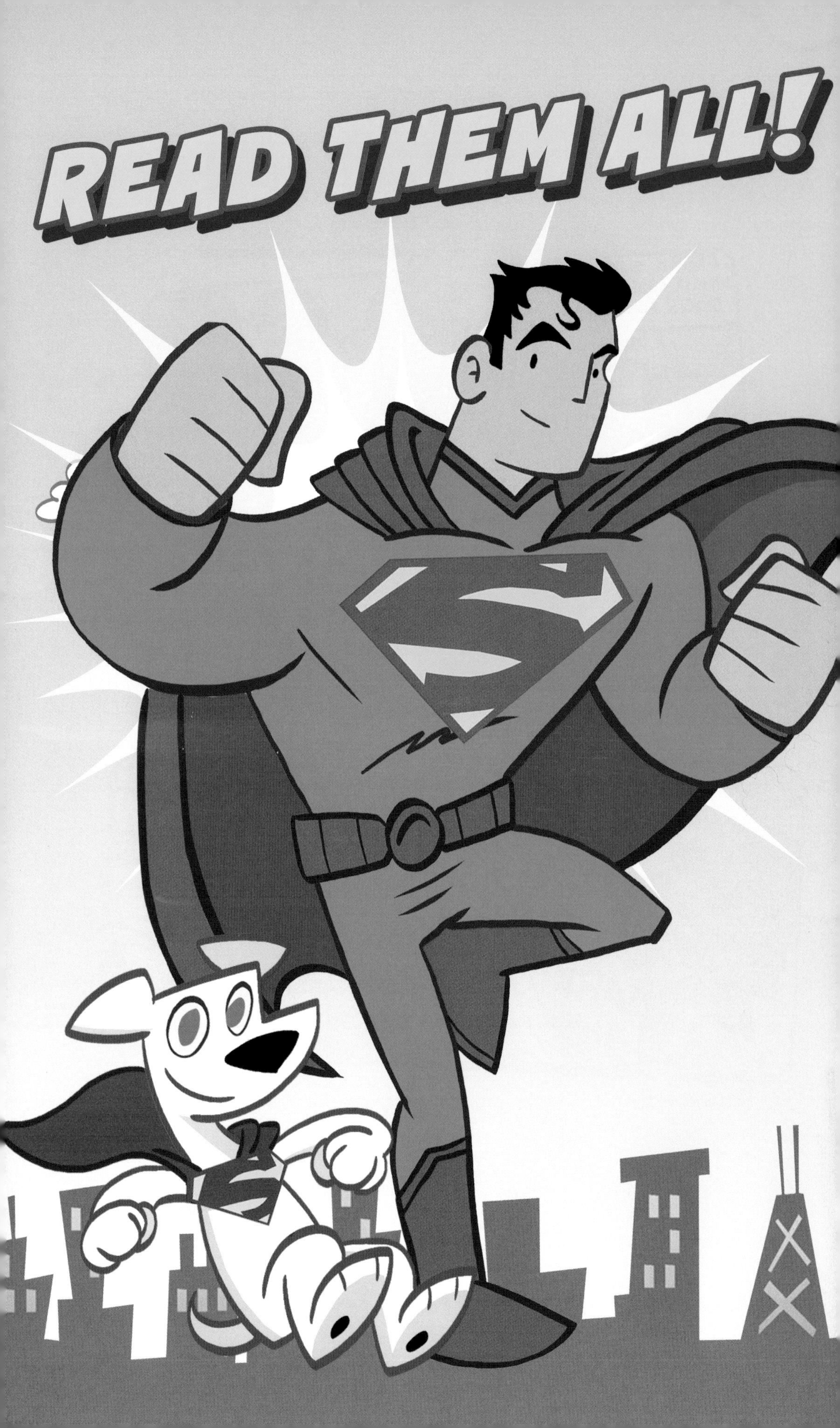
READ THEM ALL!

only from...

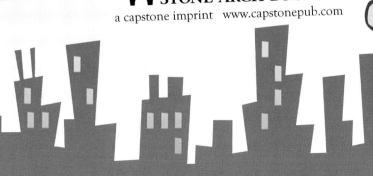

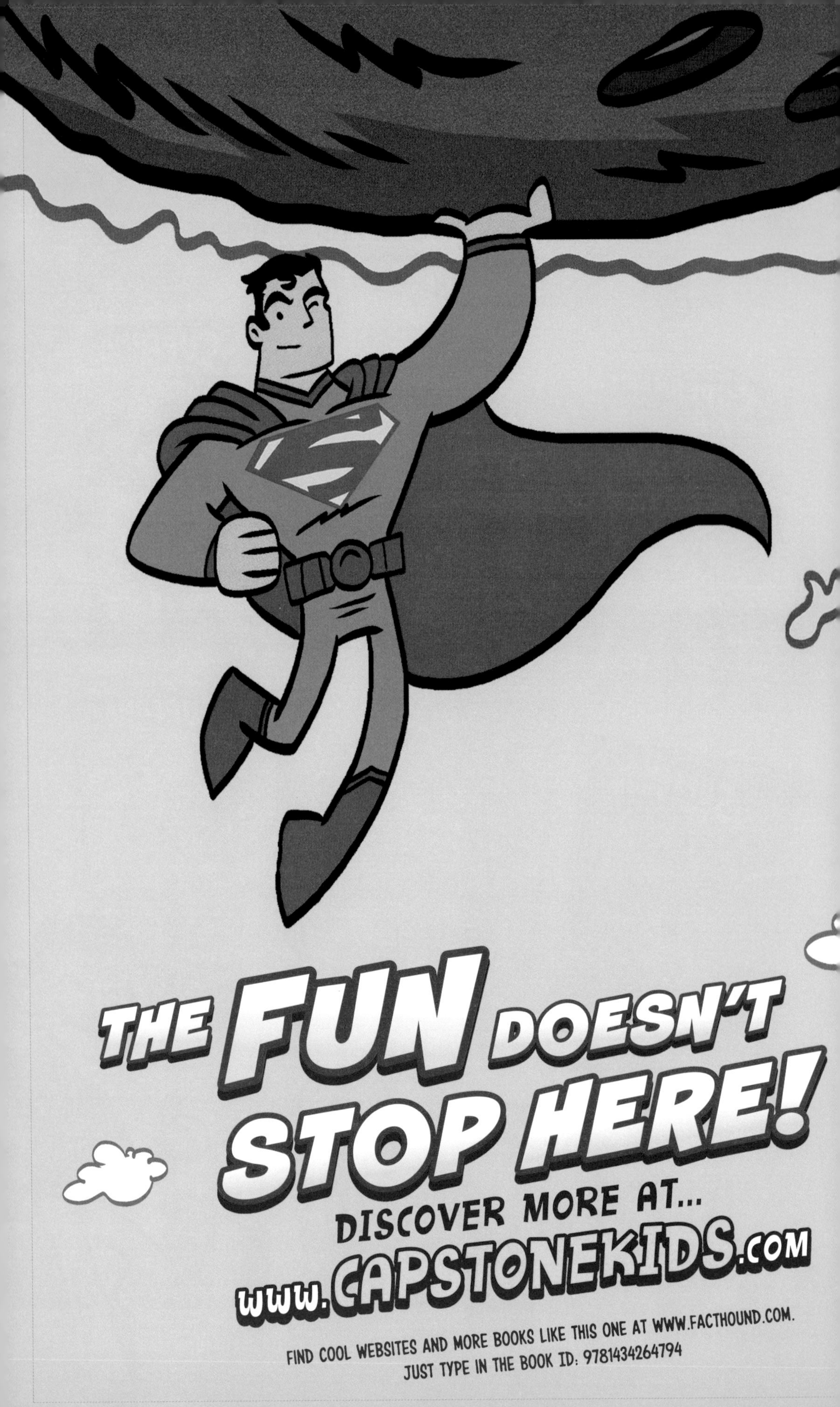